THE WATSONS
A FRAGMENT

THE JANE AUSTEN LIBRARY

The Jane Austen Library has been established
to make available rare or otherwise
unavailable editions of the novelist's work and
of the most important biographical and
critical studies. In particular, the Library will
include the authoritative texts of the juvenilia
and other smaller works and unfinished
manuscripts originally prepared by
Dr R. W. Chapman and issued by The Clarendon
Press. All the volumes in the Library will
carry a new Preface.

THE JANE AUSTEN LIBRARY

THE WATSONS
A FRAGMENT

Jane Austen

Edited by R. W. Chapman

THE ATHLONE PRESS
LONDON AND DOVER, NEW HAMPSHIRE

This reprint has been authorized by the
Oxford University Press. Reprinted from the
Clarendon Press edition 1927 by permission
of the Oxford University Press

First published in this edition 1985 by
The Athlone Press Ltd
44 Bedford Row, London WC1R 4LY
and 51 Washington Street, Dover NH 03820

Library of Congress Cataloging in Publication Data

Austen, Jane, 1775-1817.
The Watsons: a fragment.
(The Jane Austen library; 4)
I. Chapman, R. W. (Robert William), 1881-1960.
II. Title. III. Series: Austen, Jane, 1775-1817.
Selections. 1985; v. 4.
PR4034.W3   1985   823'.7   85-7352

ISBN 0-485-10503-9

Printed in Great Britain at the
University Press, Cambridge

CONTENTS

FOREWORD
by Lord David Cecil

Jane Austen does not seem to have taken either her works or herself over seriously. Certainly she showed no signs that they would be of interest to posterity. Yet now, after 150 years, she is one of the most popular of our classical novelists; more-over interest in her novels has begun to extend into interest in her. People want to know as much about her as they can, both as a writer and as a woman. The purpose of this Library is to do something to satis-fy this want.

To take the writer first: the Library will include those of her writings that were not published in her lifetime; the skits and sketches she wrote as a child, already revealing her unique character-istic humour and turn of phrase; her one unpublished novel *Lady Susan;* the two books that she never finished *The Watsons, Sanditon;* also the last chapters of *Persuasion* in their first, afterwards discarded, form. All these in their different ways tell us much about her methods of work and her judgement as to when she thought she had succeeded and failed.

Next the woman. In this section we will find descriptions of her by people who knew her, in particular her nephews and nieces; she was the most delightful and loved of aunts. There will also be accounts of places she knew well, like Bath and Lyme Regis, and her relation to them.

The final section will consist of selected biographical and critical studies of her and her work by authorities in the subject.

The Library as a whole should expand and enrich our picture of Jane Austen, woman and novelist. A homogeneous picture; for the more we learn about her the more we discover that unlike many authors, the novelist and woman are of a piece. Knowledge of one throws light on knowledge of the other; and increases our delight in them both.

PREFACE
by Brian Southam

From the completion of *Northanger Abbey* in 1799 to the commencement of *Mansfield Park* in 1811 was a period in Jane Austen's life amost empty of original work – a remarkable emptiness when we consider the years either side crowded with writing. The sole new work was *The Watsons,* a fourth novel of which no more than the opening section (about 17,500 words) was completed in a first, corrected draft before she abandoned the story in 1805.

Various theories have been advanced as to why Jane Austen gave up the novel so soon. In the *Memoir,* James Edward Austen-Leigh (who gave the untitled manuscript its name) suggested that she put it aside when she realized 'the evil of having placed her heroine too low, in such a situation of poverty and obscurity as, though not necessarily connected with vulgarity, has a sad tendency to degenerate into it'. But this is an explanation that belongs to the 1870s and, anyway, hardly fits the facts of the story, since the heroine was to refuse a peer and many a clergyman.

If we need an explanation, it is much more likely to lie in the technical problem which Jane Austen faced in telling the story of a distressed heroine, the staple character of sentimental and Gothic fiction. It is hardly surprising that at this first attempt she should meet some difficulty in appropriating this subject to her own style of domestic comedy. Alongside this literary question we also have to take account of the distress of her father's death in January 1805. According to Fanny Lefroy (a grand-daughter of James Austen) it was this event which put an end to the story.

What has come down to us, then, is a sad shadow of what might, in happier circumstances, have yielded a further novel. But the failures of genius have their small triumphs and *The Watsons* is no exception. The scene in which Emma offers to dance with the young Charles Blake is one of those poignant and eternal moments, as fine and rare as any in the completed works. Students of the novel will also value Dr Chapman's scrupulous notes on the manuscript alterations, allowing us to catch sight of the writer at work. Was *The Watsons* to be sublimated into *Emma?* That imponderable question has been raised many times. If there are clues to be found, they are here in Dr Chapman's edition, to be pursued by a new generation of palimpsest-seekers.

PREFACE

THE fragment called, by its first editor, *The Watsons*,[1] was written at some time not earlier than 1803.[2] It was first published in 1871, when the author of *A Memoir of Jane Austen by her Nephew J. E. Austen Leigh* included it in the second edition of that work. The manuscript was then in the possession of his sister. The text given by Mr. Austen Leigh has been not infrequently reprinted.

By the courtesy of the owners [3] the fragment is now reprinted from the original. The text is given as exactly as possible. The

[1] The manuscript, like that of *Sanditon*, bears no title.

[2] The watermark 1803 occurs several times. I have not detected that of 1804, which is mentioned by the first editor.

[3] The first six leaves were sold by the late William Austen Leigh at a Red Cross sale in 1918, and were lent to me in 1924 (?) by the then owner, Alice Lady Ludlow. They are now in the Pierpont Morgan Library. The remainder is the property of Mr. Austen Leigh's legatees.

privilege of collation has enabled the editor to detect some mistakes in the edition of 1871, and to restore the true reading in a few places which Mr. Austen Leigh judged it proper to modify.

In the notes are given, as far as they could be deciphered, the numerous words and phrases which were cancelled in the process of composition. The MS. in this respect closely resembles that of *Sanditon*, but is somewhat more perplexed.

The manuscript consists

(1) of a quire of two leaves, $7\frac{1}{2}$ inches by $5\frac{1}{4}$, and a quire of four leaves, $7\frac{1}{2}$ by $4\frac{3}{4}$. The watermarks are not dated.   *folios* 1–6

(2) of a series of ten quires, numbered, on the recto of each first leaf, 2 (*sic*) to 11. The leaves measure $7\frac{1}{2}$ by $4\frac{3}{4}$ (with three scraps of various sizes inserted); the folios are not numbered. Details are appended :

Quire 2 :	4 leaves, no watermark	*folios*	7–10
„ 3 :	4 leaves, no watermark	„	11–14
„ 4 :	4 leaves, no watermark	„	15–18
„ 5 :	4 leaves, watermark WS	„	19–22
„ 6 :	4 leaves, watermark WS	„	23–26

Quire 7 : 4 leaves, watermark WS,
　　　　　with a single leaf (no water-
　　　　　mark) pinned to the last of
　　　　　the quire　　　*folios* 27–30 & 30a
　,,　8 : 4 leaves, watermark 1803　*folios* 31–34
　,,　9 : 4 leaves, watermark 1803,
　　　　　with a single leaf (no water-
　　　　　mark) pinned to the first
　　　　　of the quire　　　*folios* 35–38 & 35a
　,, 10 : 4 leaves, watermark 1803,
　　　　　with a single leaf (water-
　　　　　mark not dated) pinned to
　　　　　the second of the quire

　　　　　　　　　　folios 39–42 & 40a
　,, 11 : 2 leaves, the second blank,
　　　　　watermark CURTEIS &
　　　　　SON　　　　　　　*folio* 43
　　　　　(The pins have been removed.)

THE first winter assembly in the Town
of **D.** in Surry was to be held on Tues-
day Octr ye 13th, & it was generally
expected to be a very good one ; a long
list of Country Families was confidently
run over as sure of attending, & san-
guine hopes were entertained that the
Osbornes themselves would be there.—
The Edwardes' invitation to the Watsons followed of course. The Edward's
were people of fortune who lived in the
Town & kept their coach ; the Watsons
inhabited a village about 3 miles distant, were poor & had no close carriage ; & ever since there had been
Balls in the place, the former were
accustomed to invite the Latter to dress
dine & sleep at their House, on every

2955.4　　　　B　　　　monthly

monthly return throughout the winter.
—On the present occasion, as only two
of Mr W.'s children were at home, &
one was always necessary as companion to himself, for he was sickly
& had lost his wife, one only could
profit by the kindness of their
friends; Miss Emma Watson who was
very recently returned to her family
from the care of an Aunt who had
brought her up, was to make her first
public appearance in the Neighbour-
hood; & her eldest sister, whose delight in a Ball was not lessened by a
ten years Enjoyment, had some merit
in chearfully undertaking to drive her
& all her finery in the old chair to
D. on the important morn^g.—As they
splashed along the dirty Lane Miss
Watson thus instructed & cautioned
her inexperienc'd sister.—" I dare say
it will be a very good Ball, & among so
many

many officers, you will hardly want
partners. You will find Mrs Edwards'
maid very willing to help you, and I
would advise you to ask Mary Edwards's opinion if you are at all at a
loss for she has a very good Taste.—
If Mr E. does not lose his money at
cards, you will stay as late as you can
wish for ; if he does, he will hurry you
home perhaps—but you are sure of
some comfortable soup.—I hope you
will be in good looks—.I should not be
surprised if you were to be thought one
of the prettiest girls in the room, there
is a great deal in Novelty. Perhaps
Tom Musgrave may take notice of you
—but I would advise you by all means
not to give him any encouragement.
He generally pays attention to every
new girl, but he is a great flirt & never
means anything serious." " I think I
have heard you speak of him before,
said

said Emma. Who is he?'' ''A young Man of very good fortune, quite independant, & remarkably agreable, an universal favourite wherever he goes. Most of the girls hereabouts are in love with him, or have been. I believe I am the only one among them that have escaped with a whole heart, and yet I was the first he paid attention to, when he came into this Country, six years ago; and very great attention indeed did he pay me. Some people say that he has never seemed to like any girl so well since, tho' he is always behaving in a particular way to one or another.''—

'' And how came *your* heart to be the only cold one?''—said Emma smiling. '' There was a reason for that—replied Miss W. changing colour.—I have not been very well used Emma among them, I hope you will have better luck.''—

luck."—" Dear Sister, I beg your pardon, if I have unthinkingly given you
pain."—" When first we knew Tom
Musgrave, continued Miss W. without
seeming to hear her, I was very much
attached to a young Man of the name
of Purvis a particular friend of Robert's,
who used to be with us a great deal.
Every body thought it would have been
a Match." A sigh accompanied these
words, which Emma respected in
silence—but her sister after a short
pause went on—" You will naturally
ask why it did not take place, & why
he is married to another Woman, while
I am still single.—But you must ask
him—not me—you must ask Penelope.
—Yes Emma, Penelope was at the
bottom of it all.—She thinks everything fair for a Husband; I trusted
her, she set him against me, with a
veiw of gaining him herself, & it ended
in

in his discontinuing his visits & soon after marrying somebody else.—Penelope makes light of her conduct, but *I* think such Treachery very bad. It has been the ruin of my happiness. I shall never love any Man as I loved Purvis. I do not think Tom Musgrave should be named with him in the same day."—" You quite shock me by what you say of Penelope—said Emma. Could a sister do such a thing ?—Rivalry, Treachery between sisters !—I shall be afraid of being acquainted with her—but I hope it was not so. Appearances were against her "—" You do not know Penelope.—There is nothing she w^d not do to get married—she would as good as tell you so herself.—Do not trust her with any secrets of your own, take warning by me, do not trust her ; she has her good qualities, but she has no Faith, no

Honour,

Honour, no Scruples, if she can pro-
mote her own advantage.—I wish with
all my heart she was well married.
I declare I had rather have her well-
married than myself."—" Than yourself !—Yes I can suppose so. A heart,
wounded like yours can have little inclination for Matrimony."—" Not much
indeed—but you know we must marry.
—I could do very well single for my
own part—A little Company, & a
pleasant Ball now & then, would be
enough for me, if one could be young
for ever, but my Father cannot provide
for us, & it is very bad to grow old &
be poor & laughed at.—I have lost
Purvis, it is true but very few people
marry their first Loves. I should not
refuse a man because he was not Purvis—. Not that I can ever quite forgive
Penelope."—Emma shook her head in
acquiescence.—" Penelope however has
had

had her Troubles—continued Miss W.
—she was sadly disappointed in Tom
Musgrave, who afterwards transferred
his attentions from me to her, & whom
she was very fond of ; but he never
means anything serious, & when he had
trifled with her long enough, he began
to slight her for Margaret, & poor Penelope was very wretched—. And since
then, she has been trying to make some
match at Chichester ; she wont tell us
with whom, but I beleive it is a rich
old Dr Harding, Uncle to the friend she
goes to see ;—& she has taken a vast
deal of trouble about him & given up
a great deal of Time to no purpose as
yet.—When she went away the other
day she said it should be the last time.
—I suppose you did not know what her
particular Business was at Chichester—
nor guess at the object that could take
her away, from Stanton just as you
were

were coming home after so many years absence."—" No indeed, I had not the smallest suspicion of it. I considered her engagement to Mrs Shaw just at that time as very unfortunate for me. I had hoped to find all my sisters at home; to be able to make an immediate friend of each."—" I suspect the D^r to have had an attack of the Asthma,—& that she was hurried away on that account—the Shaws are quite on her side.—At least I believe so—but she tells me nothing. She professes to keep her own counsel; she says, & truly enough, that " too many Cooks spoil the Broth ".—" I am sorry for her anxieties, said Emma,—but I do not like her plans or her opinions. I shall be afraid of her.—She must have too masculine & bold a temper.—To be so bent on Marriage—to pursue a Man merely for the sake of situation—is a

C sort

sort of thing that shocks me ; I cannot understand it. Poverty is a great Evil, but to a woman of Education & feeling it ought not, it cannot be the greatest.—I would rather be Teacher at a school (and I can think of nothing worse) than marry a Man I did not like."—" I would rather do any thing than be Teacher at a school—said her sister. *I* have been at school, Emma, & know what a Life they lead ; *you* never have.—I should not like marrying a disagreable Man any more than yourself,—but I do not think there *are* many very disagreable Men ;—I think I could like any good humoured Man with a comfortable Income.—I suppose my Aunt brought you up to be rather refined." " Indeed I do not know.— My conduct must tell you how I have been brought up. I am no judge of it myself. I cannot compare my Aunt's method

method with any other persons, because
I know no other."—But I can see in
a great many things that you are very
refined. I have observed it ever since
you came home, & I am afraid it will
not be for your happiness. Penelope
will laugh at you very much." " *That*
will not be for my happiness I am
sure.—If my opinions are wrong, I
must correct them—if they are above
my situation, I must endeavour to
conceal them.—But I doubt whether
Ridicule,—Has Penelope much wit ? "
—" Yes—she has great spirits, & never
cares what she says."—" Margaret is
more gentle I imagine ? "—" Yes—
especially in company ; she is all gentleness & mildness when anybody is
by.—But she is a little fretful & perverse among ourselves.—Poor creature!
she is possessed with the notion of Tom
Musgrave's being more seriously in
love

love with her, than he ever was with any body else, & is always expecting him to come to the point. This is the second time within this twelvemonth that she has gone to spend a month with Robert and Jane on purpose to egg him on, by her absence—but I am sure she is mistaken, & that he will no more follow her to Croydon now than he did last March.—He will never marry unless he can marry somebody very great ; Miss Osborne perhaps, or something in that stile.—" " Your account of this Tom Musgrave, Elizabeth, gives me very little inclination for his acquaintance." " You are afraid of him, I do not wonder at you." —" No indeed—I dislike & despise him."—" Dislike & Despise Tom Musgrave ! No, *that* you never can. I defy you not to be delighted with him if he takes notice of you.—I hope he will

dance

dance with you—& I dare say he will,
unless the Osbornes come with a large
party, & then he will not speak to any
body else.—'' "He seems to have
most engaging manners !—said Emma.
—Well, we shall see how irresistable
Mr Tom Musgrave & I find each other.
—I suppose I shall know him as soon
as I enter the Ball-room ; he *must*
carry some of his Charm in his face.''—
" You will not find him in the Ball-
room I can tell you, You will go early
that Mrs Edwards may get a good place
by the fire, & he never comes till late ;
& if the Osbornes are coming, he will
wait in the Passage, & come in with
them.—I should like to look in upon
you Emma. If it was but a good day
with my Father, I w^d wrap myself up,
& James should drive me over, as soon
as I had made Tea for him ; & I should
be with you by the time the Dancing
began.''

began." " What ! would you come
late at night in this Chair ? ''—" To
be sure I would.—There, I said you
were very refined ;—& *that*'s an instance of it."—Emma for a moment
made no answer—at last she said—
" I wish Elizabeth, you had not made
a point of my going to this Ball, I wish
you were going instead of me. Your
pleasure would be greater than mine.
I am a stranger here, & know nobody
but the Edwardses ; my Enjoyment
therefore must be very doubtful. Yours
among all your acquaintance w^d be
certain.—It is not too late to change.
Very little apology cd. be requisite to
the Edwardes, who must be more
glad of your company than of mine,
& I sh^d most readily return to my
Father ; & should not be at all afraid
to drive this quiet old Creature, home.
Your Cloathes I would undertake to
find

find means of sending to you."—" My dearest Emma cried Eliz: warmly—do you think I would do such a thing ?— Not for the Universe—but I shall never forget your goodnature in proposing it. You must have a sweet temper indeed ; —I never met with any thing like it !— And w^d you really give up the Ball, that I might be able to go to it !— Beleive me Emma, I am not so selfish as that comes to. No, tho' I am nine years older than you are, I would not be the means of keeping you from being seen.—You are very pretty, & it would be very hard that you should not have as fair a chance as we have all had, to make your fortune.—No Emma, whoever stays at home this winter, it shan't be you. I am sure I sh^d never have forgiven the person who kept me from a Ball at 19." Emma expressed her gratitude, & for a few minutes they
jogged

jogged on in silence.—Elizabeth first spoke.—" You will take notice who Mary Edwards dances with."—" I will remember her partners if I can—but you know they will be all strangers to me." " Only observe whether she dances with Capt. Hunter, more than once ; I have my fears in that quarter. Not that her Father or Mother like officers, but if she does you know, it is all over with poor Sam.—And I have promised to write him word who she dances with." " Is Sam. attached to Miss Edwardes ? "—" Did not you know *that* ? "—" How should I know it ? How should I know in Shropshire, what is passing of that nature in Surry ?—It is not likely that circumstances of such delicacy should make any part of the scanty communication which passed between you & me for the last 14 years ". " I wonder I never mentioned

tioned it when I wrote. Since you have
been at home, I have been so busy with
my poor Father and our great wash
that I have had no leisure to tell you
anything—but indeed I concluded you
knew it all.—He has been very much in
love with her these two years, & it is
a great disappointment to him that he
cannot always get away to our Balls—
but Mr Curtis won't often spare him,
& just now it is a sickly time at Guilford—'' " Do you suppose Miss Edwardes inclined to like him ? '' " I am
afraid not : You know she is an only
Child, & will have at least ten thousand
pounds.''—" But still she may like our
Brother.'' " Oh ! no—. The Edwardes look much higher. Her Father
& Mother w^d never consent to it. Sam
is only a Surgeon you know.—Some-
times I think she does like him. But
Mary Edwardes is rather prim &

reserved ; I do not always know what she w^d be at."—" Unless Sam feels on sure grounds with the Lady herself, It seems a pity to me that he should be encouraged to think of her at all."— " A young Man must think of some-body. said Eliz:—& why should not he be as lucky as Robert, who has got a good wife & six thousand pounds ? " " We must not all expect to be indi-vidually lucky replied Emma. The Luck of one member of a Family is Luck to all.—" " Mine is all to come I am sure—said Eliz: giving another sigh to the remembrance of Purvis.—I have been unlucky enough, & I cannot say much for you, as my Aunt married again so foolishly.—Well—you will have a good Ball I dare say. The next turning will bring us to the Turnpike. You may see the Church Tower over the hedge, & the White Hart is close by by it.—I shall long to know what you think of Tom Musgrave.'' Such were the last audible sounds of Miss Watson's voice, before they passed thro' the Turnpike gate & entered on the pitching of the Town—the jumbling & noise of which made farther Conversation most thoroughly undesirable. —The old Mare trotted heavily on, wanting no direction of the reins to take the right Turning, & making only one Blunder, in proposing to stop at the Milleners, before she drew up towards Mr Edward's door.—Mr E. lived in the best house in the Street, & the best in the place, if Mr Tomlinson the Banker might be indulged in calling his newly erected House at the end of the Town with a Shrubbery & sweep in the Country.—Mr E.s House was higher than most of its neighbours with two windows on each side the door, the

the windows guarded by posts and
chain, the door approached by a flight
of stone steps.—" Here we are—said
Eliz:—as the Carriage ceased moving—
safely arrived ;—& by the Market
Clock, we have been only five & thirty
minutes coming.—which *I* think is
doing pretty well, tho' it would be
nothing for Penelope.—Is not it a nice
Town ?—The Edwards' have a noble
house you see, & they live quite in stile.
The door will be opened by a Man in
Livery with a powder'd head, I can
tell you."

Emma had seen the Edwardses only
one morn^g at Stanton, they were therefore all but Strangers to her, & tho'
her spirits were by no means insensible
to the expected joys of the Evening, she
felt a little uncomfortable in the thought
of all that was to precede them. Her
conversation with Eliz. too giving her
some

some very unpleasant feelings, with
respect to her own family, had made
her more open to disagreable impressions from any other cause, & increased
her sense of the awkwardness of rushing
into Intimacy on so slight an acquaintance.—There was nothing in the
manners of M^{rs} or Miss Edwardes to
give immediate change to these Ideas ;
—the Mother tho' a very freindly
woman, had a reserved air, & a great
deal of formal Civility—& the daughter,
a genteel looking girl of 22, with her
hair in papers, seemed very naturally
to have caught something of the stile
of the Mother who had brought her
up.—Emma was soon left to know what
they could be, by Eliz.'s being obliged
to hurry away—& some very, very
languid remarks on the probable Brilliancy of the Ball, were all that broke
at intervals a silence of half an hour
before

before they were joined by the Master
of the house.—Mr Edwards had a
much easier, & more communicative
air than the Ladies of the Family ; he
was fresh from the Street, & he came
ready to tell what ever might interest.
—After a cordial reception of Emma,
he turned to his daughter with " Well
Mary, I bring you good news.—The
Osbornes will certainly be at the Ball
tonight.—Horses for two Carriages are
ordered from the White Hart, to be
at Osborne Castle by 9.—" " I am glad
of it—observed Mrs E., because their
coming gives a credit to our Assemblies.
The Osbornes being known to have
been at the first Ball, will dispose a
great many people to attend the
second.—It is more than they deserve,
for in fact they add nothing to the
pleasure of the Evening, they come so
late, & go so early ;—but Great People
have

have always their charm.''—M[r] Edwards proceeded to relate every other
little article of news which his morning's lounge had supplied him with, &
they chatted with greater briskness, till
M[rs] E.'s moment for dressing arrived,
& the young Ladies were carefully
recommended to lose no time.—Emma
was shewn to a very comfortable apartment, & as soon as M[rs] E.'s civilities
could leave her to herself, the happy
occupation, the first Bliss of a Ball
began.—The girls, dressing in some
measure together, grew unavoidably
better acquainted; Emma found in
Miss E.— the shew of good sense, a
modest unpretending mind, & a great
wish of obliging—& when they returned
to the parlour where M[rs] E. was sitting
respectably attired in one of the two
Sattin gowns which went thro' the
winter, & a new cap from the Mil-
liners,

liners, they entered it with much easier feelings & more natural smiles than they had taken away.—Their dress was now to be examined; Mrs Edwards acknowledged herself too old-fashioned to approve of every modern extravagance however sanctioned—& tho' complacently veiwing her daughter's good looks, w^d give but a qualified admiration; & Mr E. not less satisfied with Mary, paid some Compliments of good humoured Gallantry to Emma at her expence.—The discussion led to more intimate remarks, & Miss Edwardes gently asked Emma if she were not often reckoned very like her youngest brother.—Emma thought she could perceive a faint blush accompany the question, & there seemed something still more suspicious in the manner in which Mr E. took up the subject.— " You are paying Miss Emma no great compliment

compliment I think Mary, said he
hastily—. Mr Sam Watson is a very
good sort of young Man, & I dare say
a very clever Surgeon, but his complexion has been rather too much
exposed to all weathers, to make a likeness to him very flattering." Mary
apologized in some confusion. " She
had not thought a strong Likeness at
all incompatible with very different
degrees of Beauty.—There might be
resemblance in Countenance ; & the
complexion, & even the features be very
unlike."—" I know nothing of my
Brother's Beauty, said Emma, for I
have not seen him since he was 7 years
old—but my father reckons us alike."
" Mr Watson !—cried Mr Edwardes,
Well, you astonish me.—There is not
the least likeness in the world ; Y^r
brother's eyes are grey, yours are
brown, He has a long face, & a wide

E mouth.—

mouth.—My dear, do *you* perceive the least resemblance ?''—'' Not the least. —Miss Emma Watson puts me very much in mind of her eldest Sister, & sometimes I see a look of Miss Penelope—& once or twice there has been a glance of Mr Robert—but I cannot perceive any likeness to Mr Samuel.'' '' I see the likeness between her & Miss Watson, replied Mr E.—, very strongly —but I am not sensible of the others.— I do not much think she is like any of the Family *but* Miss Watson ; but I am very sure there is no resemblance between her & Sam.''—

This matter was settled, & they went to Dinner.—'' Your Father, Miss Emma, is one of my oldest friends—said Mr Edwardes, as he helped her to wine, when they were drawn round the fire to enjoy their Desert,—We must drink to his better health.—It is a great concern

cern to me I assure you that he should be such an Invalid.—I know nobody who likes a game of cards in a social way, better than he does ; & very few people that play a fairer rubber.—It is a thousand pities that he should be so deprived of the pleasure. For now we have a quiet little Whist club that meets three times a week at the White Hart, & if he c^d but have his health, how much he w^d enjoy it.'' '' I dare say he would Sir—& I wish with all my heart he were equal to it.'' Your Club w^d be better fitted for an Invalid, said Mrs E. if you did not keep it up so late.'' —This was an old greivance.—'' So late, my dear, what are you talking of ; cried the Husband with sturdy pleasantry—. We are always at home before Midnight. They would laugh at Osborne Castle to hear you call *that* late ; they are but just rising from dinner at midnight.''—

midnight."—"That is nothing to the
purpose.—retorted the Lady calmly.
The Osbornes are to be no rule for us.
You had better meet every night, &
break up two hours sooner." So far,
the subject was very often carried;—
but M[r] & M[rs] Edwards were so wise as
never to pass that point; & M[r] Edwards now turned to something else.—
He had lived long enough in the
Idleness of a Town to become a little
of a Gossip, & having some curiosity
to know more of the Circumstances of
his young Guest than had yet reached
him, he began with, " I think Miss
Emma, I remember your Aunt very
well about 30 years ago; I am pretty
sure I danced with her in the old rooms
at Bath, the year before I married—.
She was a very fine woman then—but
like other people I suppose she is grown
somewhat older since that time.—I
hope

hope she is likely to be happy in her second choice."

" I hope so, I beleive so, Sir—said Emma in some agitation.—" " Mr Turner had not been dead a great while I think ? " About 2 years Sir." " I forget what her name is now ? "— " O'brien." " Irish ! Ah ! I remember—& she is gone to settle in Ireland. —I do not wonder that you should not wish to go with her into *that* Country Miss Emma—. but it must be a great deprivation to her, poor Lady !—After bringing you up like a Child of her own."—" I was not so ungrateful Sir, said Emma warmly, as to wish to be any where but with her.—It did not suit them, it did not suit Capt. O'brien that I sh^d be of the party."—" Captain ! —repeated Mrs E. the Gentleman is in the army then ? " " Yes Ma'am."— " Aye—there is nothing like your officers

officers for captivating the Ladies,
Young or Old.—There is no resisting a
Cockade my dear."—" I hope there
is."—said Mrs E. gravely, with a quick
glance at her daughter ;—and Emma
had just recovered from her own perturbation in time to see a blush on
Miss E.'s cheek, & in remembering what
Elizabeth had said of Capt. Hunter, to
wonder & waver between his influence
& her brother's.—

" Elderly Ladies should be careful
how they make a second choice."
observed Mr Edwardes.—" Carefulness
—Discretion—should not be confined
to Elderly Ladies, or to a second choice
added his wife. It is quite as necessary
to young Ladies in their first."—
" Rather more so, my dear—replied he,
because young Ladies are likely to feel
the effects of it longer. When an old
Lady plays the fool, it is not in the

course

course of nature that she should suffer from it many years.'' Emma drew her hand across her eyes—& Mrs Edwards on perceiving it, changed the subject to one of less anxiety to all.—

With nothing to do but to expect the hour of setting off, the afternoon was long to the two young Ladies ; & tho' Miss Edwards was rather discomposed at the very early hour which her mother always fixed for going, that early hour itself was watched for with some eagerness.—The entrance of the Tea things at 7 o'clock was some releif— & luckily M^r & Mrs Edwards always drank a dish extraordinary, & ate an additional muffin when they were going to sit up late, which lengthened the ceremony almost to the wished for moment. At a little before 8, the Tomlinsons carriage was heard to go by, which was the constant signal for

M^{rs}

Mrs Edwards to order hers to the door ;
& in a very few minutes, the party were
transported from the quiet warmth of
a snug parlour, to the bustle, noise &
draughts of air of the broad Entrance-
passage of an Inn.—Mrs Edwards carefully guarding her own dress, while she
attended with yet greater Solicitude to
the proper security of her young
Charges' Shoulders & Throats, led the
way up the wide staircase, while no
sound of a Ball but the first Scrape
of one violin, blessed the ears of her
followers, & Miss Edwards on hazarding
the anxious enquiry of whether there
were many people come yet was told
by the Waiter as she knew she should,
that " Mr Tomlinson's family were in
the room." In passing along a short
gallery to the Assembly-room, brilliant
in lights before them, they were ac-
costed by a young Man in a morning
dress

dress & Boots, who was standing in the
doorway of a Bedchamber, apparently
on purpose to see them go by.—" Ah !
M^{rs} E— how do you do ?—How do
you do Miss E. ?—he cried, with an
easy air ;—You are determined to be
in good time I see, as usual.—The
Candles are but this moment lit "—
" I like to get a good seat by the fire
you know, Mr Musgrave." replied M^{rs}
E. " I am this moment going to dress,
said he—I am waiting for my stupid
fellow.—We shall have a famous Ball,
The Osbornes are certainly coming ;
you may depend upon *that* for I was
with Ld Osborne this morn^g—"

The party passed on—M^{rs} E's sattin
gown swept along the clean floor of the
Ball-room, to the fireplace at the upper
end, where one party only were formally
seated, while three or four Officers were
lounging together, passing in & out

from the adjoining card-room.—A very stiff meeting between these near neighbours ensued—& as soon as they were all duely placed again, Emma in the low whisper which became the solemn scene, said to Miss Edwardes, "The gentleman we passed in the passage, was Mr Musgrave, then?—He is reckoned remarkably agreable I understand.—" Miss E. answered hesitatingly—" Yes—he is very much liked by many people.—But *we* are not very intimate."—" He is rich, is not he?"—" He has about 8 or 900£ a year I beleive.—He came into possession of it, when he was very young, & my Father & Mother think it has given him rather an unsettled turn.—He is no favourite with them."—The cold & empty appearance of the Room & the demure air of the small cluster of Females at one end of it began soon to give way; the inspiriting

spiriting sound of other Carriages was heard, & continual accessions of portly Chaperons, & strings of smartly-dressed girls were received, with now & then a fresh gentleman straggler, who if not enough in Love to station himself near any fair Creature seemed glad to escape into the Card-room.—Among the increasing numbers of Military Men, one now made his way to Miss Edwards, with an air of Empressément, which decidedly said to her Companion "I am Capt. Hunter."—& Emma, who could not but watch her at such a moment, saw her looking rather distressed, but by no means displeased, & heard an engagement formed for the two first dances, which made her think her Brother Sam's a hopeless case.—

Emma in the meanwhile was not unobserved, or unadmired herself.—A
new

new face & a very pretty one, could not
be slighted—her name was whispered
from one party to another, & no sooner
had the signal been given, by the
Orchestra's striking up a favourite air,
which seemed to call the young Men to
their duty, & people the centre of the
room, than she found herself engaged
to dance with a Brother officer, introduced by Capt. Hunter.—Emma Watson was not more than of the middle
height—well made & plump, with an
air of healthy vigour.—Her skin was
very brown, but clear, smooth and
glowing— ; which with a lively Eye,
a sweet smile, & an open Countenance,
gave beauty to attract, & expression to
make that beauty improve on acquaintance.—Having no reason to be dis-
satisfied with her partner, the Even[g]
began very pleasantly to her ; & her
feelings perfectly coincided with the
re-iterated

re-iterated observation of others, that it was an excellent Ball.—The two first dances were not quite over, when the returning sound of Carriages after a long interruption, called general notice, & " the Osbornes are coming, the Osbornes are coming"—was repeated round the room.—After some minutes of extraordinary bustle without, & watchful curiosity within, the important Party, preceded by the attentive Master of the Inn to open a door which was never shut, made their appearance. They consisted of Ly. Osborne, her son Ld Osborne, her daughter Miss Osborne ; Miss Carr, her daughter's friend, Mr Howard formerly Tutor to Ld Osborne, now Clergyman of the Parish in which the Castle stood, Mrs Blake, a widow-sister who lived with him, her son a fine boy of 10 years old, & Mr Tom Musgrave ; who probably imprisoned

imprisoned within his own room, had
been listening in bitter impatience to
the sound of the Music, for the last
half hour. In their progress up the
room, they paused almost immediately
behind Emma, to receive the Compt[s]
of some acquaintance, & she heard
Ly. Osborne observe that they had
made a point of coming early for the
gratification of M[rs] Blake's little boy,
who was uncommonly fond of dancing.
—Emma looked at them all as they
passed—but chiefly & with most
interest on Tom Musgrave, who was
certainly a genteel, good looking young
man.—Of the females, Ly. Osborne
had by much the finest person ;—tho'
nearly 50, she was very handsome, &
had all the Dignity of Rank.—

L[d] Osborne was a very fine young
man ; but there was an air of Coldness,
of Carelessness, even of Awkwardness
about

about him, which seemed to speak him
out of his Element in a Ball room.
He came in fact only because it was
judged expedient for him to please the
Borough—he was not fond of Women's
company, & he never danced.—M^r
Howard was an agreable-looking Man,
a little more than Thirty.—

At the conclusion of the two Dances,
Emma found herself, she knew not
how, seated amongst the Osborne set ;
& she was immediately struck with the
fine Countenance & animated gestures
of the little boy, as he was standing
before his Mother, wondering when
they should begin.—" You will not
be surprised at Charles's impatience,
said Mrs Blake, a lively pleasant-
looking little Woman of 5 or 6 & 30,
to a Lady who was standing near her,
when you know what a partner he is
to have. Miss Osborne has been so
very

very kind as to promise to dance the two 1st dances with him.''—'' Oh! yes —we have been engaged this week. cried the boy. & we are to dance down every couple.''—On the other side of Emma, Miss Osborne, Miss Carr, & a party of young Men were standing engaged in very lively consultation— & soon afterwards she saw the smartest officer of the sett, walking off to the Orchestra to order the dance, while Miss Osborne passing before her, to her little expecting Partner hastily said— '' Charles, I beg your pardon for not keeping my engagement, but I am going to dance these two dances with Col^n Beresford. I know you will excuse me, & I will certainly dance with you after Tea.'' And without staying for an answer, she turned again to Miss Carr, & in another minute was led by Col. Beresford to begin the set.

If

If the poor little boy's face had in it's
happiness been interesting to Emma, it
was infinitely more so under this sudden
reverse ;—he stood the picture of disappointment, with crimson'd cheeks,
quivering lips, & eyes bent on the floor.
His mother, stifling her own mortification, tried to sooth his, with the prospect of Miss Osborne's second promise ;
—but tho' he contrived to utter with
an effort of Boyish Bravery " Oh ! I do
not mind it "—it was very evident by
the unceasing agitation of his features
that he minded it as much as ever.—
Emma did not think, or reflect ;—she
felt & acted—. " I shall be very happy
to dance with you Sir, if you like it."
said she, holding out her hand with the
most unaffected good humour.—The
Boy in one moment restored to all his
first delight—looked joyfully at his
Mother and stepping forwards with an

G honest

honest & simple Thank you Maam was instantly ready to attend his new acquaintance.—The Thankfulness of Mrs Blake was more diffuse ;—with a look, most expressive of unexpected pleasure, & lively Gratitude, she turned to her neighbour with repeated & fervent acknowledgements of so great & condescending a kindness to her boy.— Emma with perfect truth could assure her that she could not be giving greater pleasure than she felt herself—& Charles being provided with his gloves & charged to keep them on, they joined the Set which was now rapidly forming, with nearly equal complacency.—It was a Partnership which c^{d} not be noticed without surprise. It gained her a broad stare from Miss Osborne & Miss Carr as they passed her in the dance. "Upon my word Charles you are in luck, (said the former as she turned

turned him) you have got a better
partner than me "—to which the happy
Charles answered " Yes."—Tom Musgrave who was dancing with Miss Carr,
gave her many inquisitive glances ; &
after a time Ld Osborne himself came
& under pretence of talking to Charles,
stood to look at his partner.—Tho'
rather distressed by such observation,
Emma could not repent what she had
done, so happy had it made both the
boy & his Mother ; the latter of whom
was continually making opportunities
of addressing her with the warmest
civility.—Her little partner she found,
tho' bent cheifly on dancing, was not
unwilling to speak, when her questions
or remarks gave him anything to say ;
& she learnt, by a sort of inevitable
enquiry that he had two brothers &
a sister, that they & their Mama all
lived with his Uncle at Wickstead, that
                                    his

his Uncle taught him Latin, that he was
very fond of riding, & had a horse of
his own given him by Ld Osborne; &
that he had been out once already with
Ld Osborne's Hounds.—At the end of
these Dances Emma found they were
to drink tea;—Miss E. gave her a
caution to be at hand, in a manner
which convinced her of Mrs E.'s holding
it very important to have them both
close to her when she moved into the
Tearoom; & Emma was accordingly
on the alert to gain her proper station.
It was always the pleasure of the company to have a little bustle & croud
when they thus adjourned for refreshment;—the Tearoom was a small room
within the Cardroom, & in passing
thro' the latter, where the passage was
straightened by Tables, Mrs E. & her
party were for a few moments hemmed
in. It happened close by Lady Osborne's

borne's Cassino Table; Mr Howard
who belonged to it spoke to his
Nephew; & Emma on perceiving herself the object of attention both to
Ly. O. & him, had just turned away
her eyes in time, to avoid seeming to
hear her young companion delightedly
whisper aloud "Oh! Uncle, do look
at my partner. She is so pretty!"
As they were immediately in motion
again however Charles was hurried off
without being able to receive his
Uncle's suffrage.—On entering the Tearoom, in which two long Tables were
prepared, Ld Osborne was to be seen
quite alone at the end of one, as if
retreating as far as he could from the
Ball, to enjoy his own thoughts, & gape
without restraint.—Charles instantly
pointed him out to Emma—"There's
Lord Osborne—Let you & I go &
sit by him.—"No, no, said Emma
laughing

laughing you must sit with my friends."

Charles was now free enough to hazard a few questions in his turn. " What o'clock was it ? "—" Eleven." —" Eleven !—And I am not at all sleepy. Mama said I should be asleep before ten.—Do you think Miss Osborne will keep her word with me, when Tea is over ? " " Oh ! yes.— I suppose so."—tho' she felt that she had no better reason to give than that Miss Osborne had *not* kept it before.— " When shall you come to Osborne Castle ? "—" Never, probably.—I am not acquainted with the family." " But you may come to Wickstead & see Mama, & she can take you to the Castle.—There is a monstrous curious stuff'd Fox there, & a Badger—anybody would think they were alive. It is a pity you should not see them."—

On

On rising from Tea, there was again
a scramble for the pleasure of being
first out of the room, which happened
to be increased by one or two of the
card parties having just broken up &
the players being disposed to move
exactly the different way. Among
these was Mr Howard—his sister lean-
ing on his arm—& no sooner were they
within reach of Emma, than M^rs B.
calling her notice by a friendly touch,
said " Your goodness to Charles, my
dear Miss Watson, brings all his family
upon you. Give me leave to introduce
my Brother—Mr H.'' Emma curtsied,
the gentleman bowed—made a hasty
request for the honour of her hand in
the two next dances, to which as hasty
an affirmative was given, & they were
immediately impelled in opposite directions.—Emma was very well pleased
with the circumstance ;—there was a
quietly-

quietly-chearful, gentlemanlike air in
Mr H. which suited her—& in a few
minutes afterwards, the value of her
Engagement increased, when as she
was sitting in the Cardroom somewhat
screened by a door, she heard Ld Osborne, who was lounging on a vacant
Table near her, call Tom Musgrave
towards him & say, " Why do not you
dance with that beautiful Emma Watson ?—I want you to dance with her—
& I will come & stand by you."—" I
was determining on it this very moment
my Lord, I'll be introduced & dance
with her directly."—" Aye do—& if
you find she does not want much
Talking to, you may introduce me by
& bye."—" Very well my Lord—. If
she is like her Sisters, she will only
want to be listened to.—I will go this
moment. I shall find her in the Tea
room. That stiff old Mrs E. has never
done

done tea."—Away he went—Ld Osborne after him—& Emma lost no time
in hurrying from her corner, exactly
the other way, forgetting in her haste
that she left Mrs Edwardes behind.—
" We had quite lost you—said Mrs E.—
who followed her with Mary, in less
than five minutes.—If you prefer this
room to the other, there is no reason
why you should not be here, but we
had better all be together." Emma
was saved the Trouble of apologizing,
by their being joined at the moment by
Tom Musgrave, who requesting M^{rs} E.
aloud to do him the honour of present-
ing him to Miss Emma Watson, left
that good Lady without any choice in
the business, but that of testifying by
the coldness of her manner that she did
it unwillingly. The honour of dancing
with her, was solicited without loss of
time—& Emma, however she might

like to be thought a beautiful girl by
Lord or Commoner, was so little disposed to favour Tom Musgrave himself, that she had considerable satis-
faction in avowing her prior Engagement.—He was evidently surprised &
discomposed.—The stile of her last
partner had probably led him to beleive
her not overpowered with applications.
—" My little friend Charles Blake, he
cried, must not expect to engross you
the whole evening. We can never suffer
this—It is against the rules of the
Assembly—& I am sure it will never be
patronised by our good friend here
Mrs E. ; She is by much too nice a
judge of Decorum to give her license
to such a dangerous Particularity."—
" I am not going to dance with Master
Blake Sir." The Gentleman a little
disconcerted, could only hope he might
be more fortunate another time—&
seeming

seeming unwilling to leave her, tho'
his friend Ld Osborne was waiting in
the Doorway for the result, as Emma
with some amusement perceived—he
began to make civil enquiries after her
family.—" How comes it, that we have
not the pleasure of seeing your Sisters
here this Evening ?—Our Assemblies
have been used to be so well treated by
them, that we do not know how to take
this neglect."—" My eldest Sister is
the only one at home—& she could not
leave my Father "—" Miss Watson the
only one at home !—You astonish me !
—It seems but the day before yesterday
that I saw them all three in this Town.
But I am afraid I have been a very sad
neighbour of late. I hear dreadful com-
plaints of my negligence wherever I
go, & I confess it is a shameful length
of time since I was at Stanton.—But
I shall *now* endeavour to make myself
amends

amends for the past."—Emma's calm
curtsey in reply must have struck him
as very unlike the encouraging warmth
he had been used to receive from her
Sisters, & gave him probably the novel
sensation of doubting his own influence, & of wishing for more attention
than she bestowed. The dancing now
recommenced ; Miss Carr being impatient to *call*, everybody was required to
stand up—& Tom Musgrave's curiosity
was appeased, on seeing Mr Howard
come forward and claim Emma's hand
—" That will do as well for me "—was
Ld Osborne's remark, when his friend
carried him the news—& he was continually at Howard's Elbow during the
two dances.—The frequency of his
appearance there, was the only unpleasant part of her engagement, the
only objection she could make to M^r
Howard.—In himself, she thought him

as

as agreable as he looked ; tho' chatting
on the commonest topics he had a
sensible, unaffected, way of expressing
himself, which made them all worth
hearing, & she only regretted that he
had not been able to make his pupil's
Manners as unexceptionable as his
own.—The two dances seemed very
short, & she had her partner's au-
thority for considering them so.—At
their conclusion the Osbornes & their
Train were all on the move. "We are
off at last, said his Lordship to Tom—
How much longer do *you* stay in this
Heavenly place ?—till Sunrise ?"—
" No faith ! my Lord, I have had quite
enough of it. I assure you—I shall not
shew myself here again when I have
had the honour of attending Ly. Osborne to her Carriage. I shall retreat
in as much secrecy as possible to the
most remote corner of the House,
where

where I shall order a Barrel of Oysters,
& be famously snug." " Let us see you
soon at the Castle ; & bring me word
how she looks by daylight."—Emma
& Mrs Blake parted as old acquaintance, & Charles shook her by the
hand & wished her " goodbye " at least
a dozen times. From Miss Osborne &
Miss Carr she received something like
a jerking curtsey as they passed her ;
even Ly. Osborne gave her a look of
complacency—& his Lordship actually
came back after the others were out of
the room, to " beg her pardon ", & look
in the window seat behind her for the
gloves which were visibly compressed
in his hand.—

As Tom Musgrave was seen no more,
we may suppose his plan to have succeeded, & imagine him mortifying with
his Barrel of Oysters, in dreary solitude
—or gladly assisting the Landlady in
her

her Bar to make fresh Negus for the
happy Dancers above. Emma could
not help missing the party, by whom
she had been, tho' in some respects unpleasantly, distinguished, & the two
Dances which followed & concluded the
Ball, were rather flat, in comparison
with the others.—Mr E. having play'd
with good luck, they were some of the
last in the room—" Here we are, back
again I declare—said Emma sorrow-
fully, as she walked into the Dining
room, where the Table was prepared,
& the neat Upper maid was lighting the
Candles—" My dear Miss Edwards—
how soon it is at an end !—I wish it
could all come over again !—'' A great
deal of kind pleasure was expressed in
her having enjoyed the Even^g so much
—& Mr Edwards was as warm as herself, in praise of the fullness, brilliancy
& Spirit of the Meeting. tho' as he
had

had been fixed the whole time at the
same Table in the same Room, with
only one change of chairs, it might
have seemed a matter scarcely perceived.—But he had won 4 rubbers
out of 5, & everything went well. His
daughter felt the advantage of this
gratified state of mind, in the course
of the remarks & retrospections which
now ensued, over the welcome soup.—
" How came you not to dance with
either of the Mr Tomlinsons, Mary ?—
said her Mother. " I was always engaged when they asked me." " I
thought you were to have stood up
with Mr James, the two last dances ;
Mrs Tomlinson told me he was gone to
ask you—& I had heard you say two
minutes before that you were *not* engaged."—" Yes—but—there was a mis-
take—I had misunderstood—I did not
know I was engaged.—I thought it had
been

been for the 2 Dances after, if we staid
so long—but Capt. Hunter assured me
it was for those very Two.—"

"So, you ended with Capt. Hunter
Mary, did you?" said her Father.
And who did you begin with?"
"Capt. Hunter." was repeated, in a
very humble tone—"Hum!—That is
being constant however. But who else
did you dance with?" "Mr Norton,
& Mr Styles." "And who are they?"
"Mr Norton is a Cousin of Capt.
Hunter's."—"And who is Mr Styles?"
"One of his particular friends."—"All
in the same Reg^t added Mrs E.—Mary
was surrounded by Red coats the whole
Even^g. I should have been better
pleased to see her dancing with some
of our old Neighbours I confess.—"
"Yes, yes, we must not neglect our
old Neighbours—. But if these soldiers
are quicker than other people in a Ball

room

room, what are young Ladies to do ? "
" I think there is no occasion for their
engaging themselves so many Dances
beforehand, Mr Edwards."—" No—
perhaps not—but I remember my dear
when you & I did the same."—M^rs E.
said no more, & Mary breathed again.—
A great deal of goodhumoured pleasantry followed—& Emma went to bed in
charming Spirits, her head full of Osbornes, Blakes & Howards.—

The next morn^g brought a great
many visitors. It was the way of the
place always to call on Mrs E. on the
morn^g after a Ball, & this neighbourly
inclination was increased in the present
instance by a general spirit of curiosity
on Emma's account, as Everybody
wanted to look again at the girl who
had been admired the night before by
Ld Osborne.—

Many were the eyes, & various the
degrees

degrees of approbation with which she was examined. Some saw no fault, & some no Beauty—. With some her brown skin was the annihilation of every grace, & others could never be persuaded that she were half so handsome as Eliz: Watson had been ten years ago.—The morn^g passed quietly away in discussing the merits of the Ball with all this succession of Company—& Emma was at once astonished by finding it Two o'clock, & considering that she had heard nothing of her Father's Chair. After this discovery she had walked twice to the window to examine the Street, & was on the point of asking leave to ring the bell & make enquiries, when the light sound of a Carriage driving up to the door set her heart at ease. She stepd again to the window—but instead of the convenient but very un-smart

Family

Family Equipage perceived a neat Curricle.—Mr Musgrave was shortly afterwards announced;—& Mrs Edwards put on her very stiffest look at the sound.—Not at all dismayed however by her chilling air, he paid his Comp^{ts} to each of the Ladies with no unbecoming Ease, & continuing to address Emma, presented her a note, which he had the honour of bringing from her Sister; But to which he must observe that a verbal postscript from himself w^d be requisite.—"

The note, which Emma was beginning to read rather *before* Mrs Edwards had entreated her to use no ceremony, contained a few lines from Eliz: importing that their Father in consequence of being unusually well had taken the sudden resolution of attending the Visitation that day, & that as his Road lay quite wide from R., it

was

was impossible for her to come home till the following morn^g, unless the Edwardses w^d send her which was hardly to be expected, or she c^d meet with any chance conveyance, or did not mind walking so far.—She had scarcely run her eye thro' the whole, before she found herself obliged to listen to Tom Musgrave's farther account. " I received that note from the fair hands of Miss Watson only ten minutes ago, said he—I met her in the village of Stanton, whither my good Stars prompted me to turn my Horses heads—she was at that moment in quest of a person to employ on the Errand, & I was fortunate enough to convince her that she could not find a more willing or speedy Messenger than myself—. Remember, I say nothing of my Disinterestedness.—My reward is to be the indulgence of con-
veying

veying you to Stanton in my Curricle.—
Tho' they are not written down, I bring
your Sister's Orders for the same.—'
Emma felt distressed ; she did not like
the proposal—she did not wish to be
on terms of intimacy with the Pro-
poser—& yet fearful of encroaching on
the Edwardes', as well as wishing to go
home herself, she was at a loss how
entirely to decline what he offered—
Mrs E. continued silent, either not
understanding the case, or waiting to
see how the young Lady's inclination
lay.   Emma thanked him—but pro-
fessed herself very unwilling to give
him so much trouble.   " The Trouble
was of course, Honour, Pleasure, Delight.   What had he or his Horses to
do ? ''—Still she hesitated.   " She be-
leived she must beg leave to decline his
assistance—she was rather afraid of
the sort of carriage—.   The distance
was

was not beyond a walk.—'' Mrs E. was
silent no longer. She enquired into the
particulars—& then said '' We shall be
extremely happy Miss Emma, if you
can give us the pleasure of your company till tomorrow—but if you can not
conveniently do so, our Carriage is quite
at your Service, & Mary will be pleased
with the opportunity of seeing your
Sister.''—This was precisely what Emma had longed for ; & she accepted the
offer most thankfully ; acknowledging
that as Eliz: was entirely alone, it was
her wish to return home to dinner.—
The plan was warmly opposed by their
Visitor. '' I cannot suffer it indeed.
I must not be deprived of the happiness
of escorting you. I assure you there is
not a possibility of fear with my Horses.
You might guide them yourself. *Your
Sisters* all know how quiet they are ;
They have none of them the smallest
scruple

scruple in trusting themselves with me,
even on a Race Course.—Beleive me—
added he lowering his voice—*You* are
quite safe, the danger is only *mine*."—
Emma was not more disposed to oblige
him for all this.—" And as to M^rs
Edwardes' carriage being used the day
after a Ball, it is a thing quite out of
rule I assure you—never heard of
before—the old Coachman will look as
black as his Horses—. Won't he Miss
Edwards ? ''—No notice was taken.
The Ladies were silently firm, & the
gentleman found himself obliged to
submit.

" What a famous Ball we had last
night !—he cried, after a short pause.
How long did you keep it up, after the
Osbornes & I went away ? ''—" We had
two dances more.''—" It is making it
too much of a fatigue I think, to stay
so late.—I suppose your Set was not

a

a very full one.''—'' Yes, quite as full
as ever, except the Osbornes. There
seemed no vacancy anywhere—& everybody danced with uncommon spirit to
the very last.''—Emma said this—tho'
against her conscience.—''Indeed! perhaps I might have looked in upon you
again, if I had been aware of as much ;
—for I am rather fond of dancing than
not.—Miss Osborne is a charming girl,
is not she?'' '' I do not think her
handsome.'' replied Emma, to whom
all this was cheifly addressed. '' Perhaps she is not critically handsome,
but her Manners are delightful. And
Fanny Carr is a most interesting little
creature. You can imagine nothing
more *naive* or *piquante* ; & What do
you think of *L*^d *Osborne* Miss Watson?'' '' That he would be handsome
even, tho' he were *not* a Lord—& perhaps—better bred ; More desirous of

pleasing, & shewing himself pleased in a right place.—'' " Upon my word, you are severe upon my friend !—I assure you Ld Osborne is a very good fellow.—'' " I do not dispute his virtues—but I do not like his careless air.—'' " If it were not a breach of confidence, replied Tom with an important look, perhaps I might be able to win a more favourable opinion of poor Osborne.—'' Emma gave him no Encouragement, & he was obliged to keep his friend's secret.—He was also obliged to put an end to his visit—for Mrs Edwards' having ordered her Carriage, there was no time to be lost on Emma's side in preparing for it.—Miss Edwards accompanied her home, but as it was Dinner hour at Stanton, staid with them only a few minutes.—" Now my dear Emma, said Miss W., as soon as they were alone, you must talk to me all the

rest

rest of the day, without stopping, or
I shall not be satisfied. But first of all
Nanny shall bring in the dinner. Poor
thing !—You will not dine as you did
yesterday, for we have nothing but
some fried beef.—How nice Mary Edwards looks in her new pelisse !—And
now tell me how you like them all, &
what I am to say to Sam. I have begun
my letter, Jack Stokes is to call for it
tomorrow, for his Uncle is going within
a mile of Guilford the next day.—"
Nanny brought in the dinner ;—" We
will wait upon ourselves, continued
Eliz: & then we shall lose no time.—
And so, you would not come home with
Tom Musgrave ?"—" No. You had
said so much against him that I could
not wish either for the obligation, or
the Intimacy which the use of his
Carriage must have created—. I should
not even have liked the appearance of
it

it.—" " You did very right ; tho' I
wonder at your forbearance, & I do
not think I could have done it myself.—
He seemed so eager to fetch you, that
I could not say no, tho' it rather went
against me to be throwing you together,
so well as I knew his Tricks ;—but I
did long to see you, & it was a clever
way of getting you home ; Besides it
won't do to be too nice.—Nobody could
have thought of the Edwards' letting
you have their Coach,—after the Horses
being out so late.—But what am I to
say to Sam ? ''—" If you are guided by
me, you will not encourage him to
think of Miss Edwards.—The Father is
decidedly against him, the Mother shews
him no favour, & I doubt his having
any interest with Mary. She danced
twice with Capt. Hunter, & I think
shews him in general as much Encouragement as is consistent with her
disposition

disposition, & the circumstances she is placed in.—She once mentioned Sam, & certainly with a little confusion—but that was perhaps merely oweing to the consciousness of his liking her, which may very probably have come to her knowledge."—" Oh ! dear Yes—she has heard enough of that from us all. Poor Sam !—He is out of luck as well as other people.—For the life of me Emma, I cannot help feeling for those that are cross'd in Love.—Well—now begin, & give me an account of everything as it happened.—'' Emma obeyed her—& Eliz: listened with very little interruption till she heard of Mr H. as a partner.—" Dance with Mr H.—Good Heavens ! You don't say so ! Why—he is quite one of the great & Grand ones ;—Did not you find him very high ? ''—" His manners are of a kind to give *me* much more Ease & confidence

confidence than Tom Musgrave's."
" Well—go on. I should have been
frightened out of my wits, to have had
anything to do with the Osborne's
set."—Emma concluded her narration.
—" And so, you really did not dance
with Tom M. at all ?—But you must
have liked him, you must have been
struck with him altogether."—" I do
not like him, Eliz:—. I allow his person
& air to be good—& that his manners
to a certain point—his address rather—
is pleasing.—But I see nothing else to
admire in him.—On the contrary, he
seems very vain, very conceited, ab-
surdly anxious for Distinction, & absolutely contemptible in some of the
measures he takes for becoming so.—
There is a ridiculousness about him
that entertains me—but his company
gives me no other agreable Emotion."
" My dearest Emma !—You are like
nobody

nobody else in the World.—It is well
Margaret is not by.—You do not offend
me, tho' I hardly know how to beleive
you. But Marg^t w^d never forgive such
words." "I wish Marg^t could have
heard him profess his ignorance of her
being out of the Country; he declared
it seemed only two days since he had
seen her.—" "Aye—that is just like
him. & yet this is the Man, she *will*
fancy so desperately in love with her.—
He is no favourite of mine, as you well
know, Emma;—but you must think
him agreable. Can you lay your
hand on your heart, & say you do
not?"—"Indeed I can. Both Hands;
& spread to their widest extent."—
"I should like to know the Man you
do think agreable." "His name is
Howard." "Howard! Dear me. I
cannot think of *him*, but as playing
cards with Ly Osborne, & looking
proud.

proud.—I must own however that it *is* a releif to me, to find you can speak as you do, of Tom Musgrave ; my heart did misgive me that you would like him too well. You talked so stoutly beforehand, that I was sadly afraid your Brag would be punished.—I only hope it will last ;—& that he will not come on to pay you much attention ; it is a hard thing for a woman to stand against the flattering ways of a Man, when he is bent upon pleasing her.—"
As their quietly-sociable little meal concluded, Miss Watson could not help observing how comfortably it had passed. " It is so delightful to me, said she, to have Things going on in peace & goodhumour. Nobody can tell how much I hate quarrelling. Now, tho' we have had nothing but fried beef, how good it has all seemed.—I wish everybody were as easily satisfied

as

as you—but poor Marg^t is very snap-
pish, & Penelope owns she had rather
have Quarrelling going on, than nothing
at all."—Mr Watson returned in the
Evening, not the worse for the exertion
of the day, & consequently pleased with
what he had done, & glad to talk of it,
over his own Fireside.—

Emma had not foreseen any interest
to herself in the occurrences of a Visitation—but when she heard Mr Howard
spoken of as the Preacher, & as having
given them an excellent Sermon, she
could not help listening with a quicker
Ear.—" I do not know when I have
heard a Discourse more to my mind—
continued Mr W. or one better delivered.
—He reads extremely well, with great
propriety & in a very impressive
manner ; & at the same time without
any Theatrical grimace or violence.—
I own, I do not like much action in the

2955.4   L   pulpit

pulpit—I do not like the studied air &
artificial inflexions of voice, which your
very popular & most admired Preachers
generally have.—A simple delivery is
much better calculated to inspire Devotion, & shews a much better Taste.—
Mr H. read like a scholar & a gentleman."—" And what had you for dinner
Sir ? "—said his eldest Daughter.—
He related the Dishes & told what he
had ate himself. " Upon the whole, he
added, I have had a very comfortable
day ; my old friends were quite surprised to see me amongst them—& I
must say that everybody paid me great
attention, & seemed to feel for me as
an Invalid.—They would make me sit
near the fire, & as the partridges were
pretty high, Dr Richards would have
them sent away to the other end of
the Table, that they might not offend
Mr Watson—which I thought very
kind

kind of him.—But what pleased me as much as anything was Mr Howard's attention ;—There is a pretty steep flight of steps up to the room we dine in—which do not quite agree with my gouty foot—& Mr Howard walked by me from the bottom to the top, & would make me take his arm.—It struck me as very becoming in so young a Man, but I am sure I had no claim to expect it ; for I never saw him before in my Life.—By the bye, he enquired after one of my Daughters, but I do not know which. I suppose you know among yourselves."—

On the 3^d day after the Ball, as Nanny at five minutes before three, was beginning to bustle into the parlour with the Tray & the Knife-case, she was suddenly called to the front door, by the sound of as smart a rap as the end

of

of a riding-whip c^d give—& tho' charged
by Miss W. to let nobody in, returned in
half a minute, with a look of awkward
dismay, to hold the parlour door open
for Ld Osborne & Tom Musgrave.—
The surprise of the young Ladies may
be imagined. No visitors would have
been welcome at such a moment; but
such visitors as these—such a one as
Ld Osborne at least, a nobleman & a
stranger, was really distressing.—He
looked a little embarrassed himself,—
as, on being introduced by his easy,
voluble friend, he muttered something
of doing himself the honour of waiting
on Mr Watson.—Tho' Emma could not
but take the compliment of the visit to
herself, she was very far from enjoying
it. She felt all the inconsistency of such
an acquaintance with the very humble
stile in which they were obliged to live ;
& having in her Aunt's family been
used

used to many of the Elegancies of Life,
was fully sensible of all that must be
open to the ridicule of Richer people in
her present home.—Of the pain of such
feelings, Eliz: knew very little ;—her
simpler Mind, or juster reason saved
her from such mortification—& tho'
shrinking under a general sense of Inferiority, she felt no particular Shame.—
Mr Watson, as the Gentlemen had
already heard from Nanny, was not
well enough to be down stairs ;—With
much concern they took their seats—
Ld. Osborne near Emma, & the convenient Mr Musgrave in high spirits at
his own importance, on the other side
of the fireplace with Elizth.—*He* was
at no loss for words ;—but when Ld.
Osborne had hoped that Emma had
not caught cold at the Ball, he had
nothing more to say for some time,
& could only gratify his Eye by occa-
sional

sional glances at his fair neighbour.—
Emma was not inclined to give herself
much trouble for his Entertainment—&
after hard labour of mind, he produced the remark of it's being a
very fine day, & followed it up with
the question of, "Have you been
walking this morning?" "No, my
Lord. We thought it too dirty."
"You should wear half-boots."—After
another pause, "Nothing sets off a
neat ancle more than a half-boot;
nankin galoshed with black looks very
well.—Do not you like Half-boots?
"Yes—but unless they are so stout as
to injure their beauty, they are not
fit for Country walking."—"Ladies
should ride in dirty weather.—Do you
ride?" "No my Lord." "I wonder
every Lady does not.—A woman never
looks better than on horseback.—"
"But every woman may not have the
inclination

inclination, or the means." "If they knew how much it became them, they would all have the inclination—& I fancy Miss Watson—when once they had the inclination, the means w^d soon follow."—"Your Lordship thinks we always have our own way.—*That* is a point on which Ladies & Gentle^n have long disagreed—But without pretending to decide it, I may say that there are some circumstances which even *Women* cannot controul.—Female Economy will do a great deal my Lord, but it cannot turn a small income into a large one."—Ld Osborne was silenced. Her manner had been neither sententious nor sarcastic, but there was a something in it's mild seriousness, as well as in the words themselves which made his Lordship think ;—and when he addressed her again, it was with a degree of considerate propriety,

totally

totally unlike the half-awkward, half-
fearless stile of his former remarks.—
It was a new thing with him to wish
to please a woman; it was the first
time that he had ever felt what was due
to a woman, in Emma's situation.—
But as he wanted neither Sense nor
a good disposition, he did not feel it
without effect.—" You have not been
long in this Country I understand,
said he in the tone of a Gentle^{n}.
I hope you are pleased with it."—He
was rewarded by a gracious answer,
& a more liberal full veiw of her face
than she had yet bestowed. Unused
to exert himself, & happy in contem-
plating her, he then sat in silence for
some minutes longer, while Tom Musgrave was chattering to Elizth, till they
were interrupted by Nanny's approach,
who half opening the door & putting
in her head, said " Please Ma'am,
Master

Master wants to know why he be'nt
to have his dinner."—The Gentlemen,
who had hitherto disregarded every
symptom, however positive, of the near-
ness of that Meal, now jumped up
with apologies, while Elizth called
briskly after Nanny " to tell Betty to
take up the Fowls."—" I am sorry it
happens so—she added, turning goodhumouredly towards Musgrave—but
you know what early hours we keep.—"
Tom had nothing to say for himself,
he knew it very well, & such honest
simplicity, such shameless Truth rather
bewildered him.—Ld Osborne's parting
Comp^{ts} took some time, his inclination
for speech seeming to increase with the
shortness of the term for indulgence.—
He recommended Exercise in defiance
of dirt—spoke again in praise of Half-
boots—begged that his Sister might
be allow'd to send Emma the name of

M   her

her Shoemaker—& concluded with saying, " My Hounds will be hunting this
Country next week—I beleive they will
throw off at Stanton Wood on Wednes-
day at 9 o'clock.—I mention this, in
hopes of y^r being drawn out to see
what's going on.—If the morning's
tolerable, pray do us the honour of
giving us your good wishes in person.—

The Sisters looked on each other
with astonishment, when their Visitors
had withdrawn. " Here's an unac-
countable Honour ! cried Eliz: at last.
Who would have thought of Ld Osborne's coming to Stanton.—He is very
handsome—but Tom Musgrave looks
all to nothing, the smartest & most
fashionable Man of the two. I am
glad he did not say anything to me ;
I w^d not have had to talk to such a
great Man for the world. Tom was
very agreable, was not he ?—But did
                                    you

you hear him ask where Miss Penelope
& Miss Marg^t were, when he first came
in ?—It put me out of patience.—I am
glad Nanny had not laid the Cloth
however, it w^d have looked so awkward;
—just the Tray did not signify.—"
To say that Emma was not flattered
by Ld Osborne's visit, would be to
assert a very unlikely thing, & de-
scribe a very odd young Lady; but
the gratification was by no means
unalloyed; His coming was a sort of
notice which might please her vanity,
but did not suit her pride, & she w^d
rather have known that he wished
the visit without presuming to make
it, than have seen him at Stanton.—
Among other unsatisfactory feelings
it once occurred to her to wonder
why Mr Howard had not taken the
same privilege of coming, & accompanied his Lordship—but she was
willing

willing to suppose that he had either known nothing about it, or had declined any share in a measure which carried quite as much Impertinence in it's form as Goodbreeding.—M^r W was very far from being delighted, when he heard what had passed ;—a little peevish under immediate pain, & ill disposed to be pleased, he only replied—" Phoo ! Phoo !—What occasion could there be for Ld O.'s coming. I have lived here 14 years without being noticed by any of the family. It is some foolery of that idle fellow T. Musgrave. I cannot return the visit.—*I* would not if I could. And when T. Musgrave was met with again, he was commissioned with a message of excuse to Osborne Castle, on the too-sufficient plea of Mr Watson's infirm state of health.—

A week or ten days rolled quietly away after this visit, before any new bustle

bustle arose to interrupt even for half
a day, the tranquil & affectionate intercourse of the two Sisters, whose mutual
regard was increasing with the intimate
knowledge of each other which such
intercourse produced.—The first circumstance to break in on this serenity,
was the receipt of a letter from Croydon
to announce the speedy return of Margaret, & a visit of two or three days
from M^r & Mrs Robert Watson, who
undertook to bring her home & wished
to see their Sister Emma.—It was an
expectation to fill the thoughts of the
Sisters at Stanton, & to busy the hours
of one of them at least—for as Jane
had been a woman of fortune, the
preparations for her entertainment were
considerable, & as Eliz: had at all
times more good will than method in
her guidance of the house, she could
make no change without a Bustle.—

An

An absence of 14 years had made all her Brothers & Sisters Strangers to Emma, but in her expectation of Margaret there was more than the awkwardness of such an alienation; she had heard things which made her dread her return; & the day which brought the party to Stanton seemed to her the probable conclusion of almost all that had been comfortable in the house.— Robert Watson was an Attorney at Croydon, in a good way of Business; very well satisfied with himself for the same, & for having married the only daughter of the Attorney to whom he had been Clerk, with a fortune of six thousand pounds.—Mrs Robt was not less pleased with herself for having had that six thousand pounds, & for being now in possession of a very smart house in Croydon, where she gave genteel parties, & wore fine cloathes.—In her person

person there was nothing remarkable;
her manners were pert & conceited.—
Margaret was not without beauty;
she had a slight, pretty figure, &
rather wanted Countenance than good
features;—but the sharp & anxious
expression of her face made her beauty
in general little felt.—On meeting her
long-absent Sister, as on every occasion
of shew, her manner was all affection
& her voice all gentleness; continual
smiles & a very slow articulation being
her constant resource when determined
on pleasing.—

She was now so " delighted to see
dear, dear Emma " that she could
hardly speak a word in a minute.—
" I am sure we shall be great friends "
—she observed, with much sentiment,
as they were sitting together.—Emma
scarcely knew how to answer such a
proposition—& the manner in which it

was

was spoken, she could not attempt to equal. Mrs R.W. eyed her with much familiar curiosity & Triumphant Compassion;—the loss of the Aunt's fortune was uppermost in her mind, at the moment of meeting ;—& she cd. not but feel how much better it was to be the daughter of a gentleman of property in Croydon, than the neice of an old woman who threw herself away on an Irish Captain.—Robert was carelessly kind, as became a prosperous Man & a brother ; more intent on settling with the Post-Boy, inveighing against the Exorbitant advance in Posting, & pondering over a doubtful halfcrown, than on welcoming a Sister, who was no longer likely to have any property for him to get the direction of.—" Your road through the village is infamous, Eliz: ; said he, worse than ever it was. By Heaven ! I would endite it if I lived

lived near you. Who is Surveyor now?''—There was a little neice at Croydon, to be fondly enquired after by the kind-hearted Elizabeth, who regretted very much her not being of the party.—" You are very good—replied her Mother—& I assure you it went very hard with Augusta to have us come away without her. I was forced to say we were only going to Church & promise to come back for her directly.—But you know it would not do, to bring her without her maid, & I am as particular as ever in having her properly attended to." " Sweet little Darling !—cried Marg*—It quite broke my heart to leave her.—" " Then why was you in such a hurry to run away from her ? cried Mrs R.—You are a sad shabby girl.—I have been quarrelling with you all the way we came, have not I ?—Such a visit

as this, I never heard of !—You know how glad we are to have any of you with us—if it be for months together.— & I am sorry, (with a witty smile) we have not been able to make Croydon agreable this autumn.''—'' My dearest Jane—do not overpower me with your Raillery.—You know what induce-ments I had to bring me home,—spare me, I entreat you—. I am no match for your arch sallies.—'' '' Well, I only beg you will not set your Neighbours against the place.—Perhaps Emma may be tempted to go back with us, & stay till Christmas, if you don't put in your word.''—Emma was greatly obliged. '' I assure you we have very good society at Croydon.—I do not much attend the Balls, they are rather too mixed,—but our parties are very select & good.—I had seven Tables last week in my Drawingroom.—Are you
fond

fond of the Country ? How do you like
Stanton ? ''—'' Very much ''—replied
Emma, who thought a comprehensive
answer, most to the purpose.—She saw
that her Sister in law despised her
immediately.—Mrs R. W. was indeed
wondering what sort of a home Emma
c^d possibly have been used to in
Shropshire, & setting it down as certain
that the Aunt could never have had
six thousand pounds.—'' How charming Emma is !—'' whispered Marg^t to
Mrs Robert in her most languishing
tone.—Emma was quite distress'd by
such behaviour ;—& she did not like it
better when she heard Marg^t 5 minutes
afterwards say to Eliz: in a sharp quick
accent, totally unlike the first—'' Have
you heard from Pen. since she went to
Chichester ?—I had a letter the other
day.—I don't find she is likely to
make anything of it. I fancy she'll
come

come back ' Miss Penelope ' as she
went.—''

Such, she feared would be Margaret's
common voice, when the novelty of
her own appearance were over; the
tone of artificial Sensibility was not
recommended by the idea.—The Ladies
were invited upstairs to prepare for
dinner. " I hope you will find things
tolerably comfortable Jane ''—said
Eliz[th] as she opened the door of the
spare bedchamber.—" My good creature, replied Jane, use no ceremony
with me, I intreat you. I am one of
those who always take things as they
find them. I hope I can put up with
a small apartment for two or three
nights, without making a peice of
work. I always wish to be treated
quite " en famille " when I come to
see you—& now I do hope you have
not been getting a great dinner for us.
—Remember

—Remember we never eat suppers."—
" I suppose, said Marg^t rather quickly
to Emma, you & I are to be together ;
Elizth always takes care to have a room
to herself."—" No—Elizth gives me half
her's."—" Oh !—(in a soften'd voice, &
rather mortified to find that she was
not ill used) " I am sorry I am not to
have the pleasure of your company—
especially as it makes me nervous to be
much alone."

Emma was the first of the females in
the parlour again ; on entering it she
found her brother alone.—" So Emma,
said he, you are quite the Stranger at
home. ˋIt must seem odd enough to
you to be here.—A pretty peice of
work your Aunt Turner has made of
it !—By Heaven ! A woman should
never be trusted with money. I always
said she ought to have settled something on you, as soon as her Husband
died

died.'' '' But that would have been
trusting *me* with money, replied Emma,
& *I* am a woman too.—'' '' It might
have been secured to your future use,
without your having any power over
it now.—What a blow it must have
been upon you !—To find yourself,
instead of Heiress of 8 or 9000 £, sent
back a weight upon your family, without a sixpence.—I hope the old woman
will smart for it.'' '' Do not speak
disrespectfully of her—She was very
good to me ; & if she has made an
imprudent choice, she will suffer more
from it herself, than *I* can possibly
do.'' '' I do not mean to distress you,
but you know every body must think
her an old fool.—I thought Turner had
been reckoned an extraordinary sensible, clever man.—How the Devil came
he to make such a will ? ''—'' My
Uncle's sense is not at all impeached in
my

my opinion, by his attachment to my Aunt. She had been an excellent wife to him. The most Liberal & enlightened Minds are always the most confiding.— The event has been unfortunate, but my Uncle's memory is if possible endeared to me by such a proof of tender respect for my Aunt."—" That's odd sort of Talking!—He might have provided decently for his widow, without leaving every thing that he had to dispose of, or any part of it at her mercy.—" My Aunt may have erred— said Emma warmly—she *has* erred— but my Uncle's conduct was faultless. I was her own Neice, & he left to herself the power & the pleasure of providing for me."—" But unluckily she has left the pleasure of providing for you, to your Father, & without the power.— That's the long & the short of the business. After keeping you at a distance
from

from your family for such a length of
time as must do away all natural
affection among us & breeding you up
(I suppose) in a superior stile, you are
returned upon their hands without a
sixpence.'' '' You know, replied Emma
struggling with her tears, my Uncle's
melancholy state of health.—He was
a greater Invalid than my father. He
c^d not leave home.'' '' I do not mean
to make you cry.—said Robt rather
softened—& after a short silence, by
way of changing the subject, he added
—'' I am just come from my Father's
room, he seems very indifferent. It
will be a sad break-up when he dies.
Pity, you can none of you get married !—You must come to Croydon as
well as the rest, & see what you can
do there.—I beleive if Marg^t had had
a thousand or fifteen hundred pounds,
there was a young man who w^d have
thought

thought of her." Emma was glad
when they were joined by the others ;
it was better to look at her Sister in
law's finery than listen to Robert, who
had equally irritated & greived her.—
Mrs Robert exactly as smart as she had
been at her own party, came in with
apologies for her dress—" I would not
make you wait, said she, so I put on
the first thing I met with.—I am afraid
I am a sad figure.—My dear Mr W.—
(to her husband) you have not put any
fresh powder in your hair."—" No—
I do not intend it.—I think there is
powder enough in my hair for my wife
& sisters.—" " Indeed you ought to
make some alteration in your dress
before dinner when you are out visitting,
tho' you do not at home." " Nonsense."—" It is very odd you should
not like to do what other gentlemen
do. Mr Marshall & Mr Hemmings

change their dress every day of their Lives before dinner. And what was the use of my putting up your last new Coat, if you are never to wear it." —" Do be satisfied with being fine yourself, & leave your husband alone." —To put an end to this altercation, & soften the evident vexation of her sister in law, Emma (tho' in no Spirits to make such nonsense easy) began to admire her gown.—It produced immediate complacency.—" Do you like it ? —said she.—I am very happy.—It has been excessively admired ;—but sometimes I think the pattern too large.— I shall wear one tomorrow that I think you will prefer to this.—Have you seen the one I gave Margaret ?"—

Dinner came, & except when Mrs R. looked at her husband's head, she continued gay & flippant, chiding Elizth for the profusion on the Table, & absolutely

absolutely protesting against the entrance of the roast Turkey—which
formed the only exception to " You
see your dinner".—" I do beg &
entreat that no Turkey may be seen
today. I am really frightened out of
my wits with the number of dishes we
have already. Let us have no Turkey
I beseech you."—" My dear, replied
Eliz. the Turkey is roasted, & it may
just as well come in, as stay in the
Kitchen. Besides if it is cut, I am in
hopes my Father may be tempted to
eat a bit, for it is rather a favourite
dish." " You may have it in my dear,
but I assure you I shan't touch it."—

Mr Watson had not been well enough
to join the party at dinner, but was
prevailed on to come down & drink
tea with them.—" I wish we may be
able to have a game of cards tonight,"
said Eliz. to Mrs R. after seeing her
father

father comfortably seated in his arm
chair.—" Not on my account my dear,
I beg. You know I am no card player.
I think a snug chat infinitely better. I
always say cards are very well sometimes, to break a formal circle, but one
never wants them among friends."
" I was thinking of it's being something
to amuse my father, answered Eliz^th—
if it was not disagreable to you.
He says his head won't bear Whist—
but perhaps if we make a round game
he may be tempted to sit down with
us."—" By all means my dear Creature.
I am quite at your service. Only do
not oblige me to chuse the game, that's
all. *Speculation* is the only round game
at Croydon now, but I can play anything.—When there is only one or two
of you at home, you must be quite at
a loss to amuse him—why do not you
get him to play at Cribbage ?—Margaret

garet & I have played at Cribbage, most
nights that we have not been engaged.''
—A sound like a distant Carriage was
at this moment caught; everybody
listened; it became more decided; it
certainly drew nearer.—It was an un-
usual sound in Stanton at any time
of the day, for the Village was on no
very public road, & contained no gentleman's family but the Rector's.—
The wheels rapidly approached;—in
two minutes the general expectation
was answered; they stopped beyond
a doubt at the garden gate of the Parsonage. " Who could it be ?—it was
certainly a postchaise.—Penelope was
the only creature to be thought of.
She might perhaps have met with some
unexpected opportunity of returning.''
—A pause of suspense ensued.—Steps
were distinguished, first along the
paved Footway which led under the
windows

windows of the house to the front door, & then within the passage. They were the steps of a Man. It could not be Penelope. It must be Samuel.—The door opened, & displayed Tom Musgrave in the wrap of a Travellor.—He had been in London & was now on his way home, & he had come half a mile out of his road merely to call for ten minutes at Stanton. He loved to take people by surprise, with sudden visits at extraordinary seasons ; & in the present instance had had the additional motive of being able to tell the Miss Watsons, whom he depended on finding sitting quietly employed after tea, that he was going home to an 8 o'clock dinner.—As it happened however, he did not give more surprise than he received, when instead of being shewn into the usual little sitting room, the door of the best parlour a foot larger

each

each way than the other was thrown
open, & he beheld a circle of smart people
whom he c^d not immediately recognise
arranged with all the honours of visit-
ing round the fire, & Miss Watson
sitting at the best Pembroke Table,
with the best Tea things before her.
He stood a few seconds, in silent amaze-
ment. — " Musgrave ! " — ejaculated
Margaret in a tender voice.—He recol-
lected himself, & came forward, delighted to find such a circle of Friends,
& blessing his good fortune for the
unlooked-for Indulgence.—He shook
hands with Robert, bowed & smiled to
the Ladies, & did everything very
prettily ; but as to any particularity of
address or Emotion towards Margaret,
Emma who closely observed him, perceived nothing that did not justify
Eliz.'s opinions tho' Margaret's modest
smiles imported that she meant to
take

take the visit to herself.—He was persuaded without much difficulty to throw off his greatcoat, & drink tea with them. "For whether he dined at 8 or 9, as he observed, was a matter of very little consequence."—and without seeming to seek, he did not turn away from the chair close to Margaret which she was assiduous in providing him.—She had thus secured him from her Sisters—but it was not immediately in her power to preserve him from her Brother's claims, for as he came avowedly from London, & had left it only 4. hours ago, the last current report as to public news, & the general opinion of the day must be understood, before Robert could let his attention be yeilded to the less national, & important demands of the Women.—At last however he was at liberty to hear Margaret's soft address, as she spoke

her

her fears of his having had a most
terrible, cold, dark dreadful Journey.—
" Indeed you should not have set out
so late.—" " I could not be earlier, he
replied. I was detained chatting at
the Bedford, by a friend.—All hours
are alike to me.—How long have you
been in the Country Miss Marg^t ? "—
" We came only this morn^g.—My
kind Brother & Sister brought me home
this very morn^g.—'Tis singular is not
it ? " " You were gone a great while,
were not you ? a fortnight I suppose ? "—" *You* may call a fortnight
a great while Mr Musgrave, said M^{rs}
Robert smartly—but *we* think a month
very little. I assure you we bring her
home at the end of a month, much
against our will." " A month ! have
you really been gone a month ! 'tis
amazing how Time flies.—" " You
may imagine, said Marg^t in a sort of

Whisper, what are my Sensations in
finding myself once more at Stanton.
You know what a sad visitor I make.—
And I was so excessively impatient to
see Emma ;—I dreaded the meeting, &
at the same time longed for it.—Do
not you comprehend the sort of feeling ?''—'' Not at all, cried he aloud.
I could never dread a meeting with
Miss Emma Watson,—or any of her
Sisters.'' It was lucky that he added
that finish.—'' Were you speaking to
me ?''—said Emma, who had caught
her own name.—'' Not absolutely—he
answered—but I was thinking of you,
—as many at a greater distance are
probably doing at this moment.—Fine
open weather Miss Emma !—Charming
season for Hunting.'' '' Emma is delightful, is not she ?—whispered Marg^t.
I have found her more than answer my
warmest hopes.—Did you ever see
anything

anything more perfectly beautiful ?—
I think even *you* must be a convert to
a brown complexion.''—He hesitated ;
Margaret was fair herself, & he did not
particularly want to compliment her ;
but Miss Osborne & Miss Carr were likewise fair, & his devotion to them carried
the day. " Your Sister's complexion,
said he at last, is as fine as a dark
complexion can be, but I still profess
my preference of a white skin. You
have seen Miss Osborne ?—she is my
model for a truly feminine complexion,
& she is very fair.''—" Is she fairer
than me ? ''—Tom made no reply.—
" Upon my Honour Ladies, said he,
giving a glance over his own person,
I am highly endebted to your Con-
descension for admitting me, in such
Dishabille into your Drawing room. I
really did not consider how unfit I was
to be here or I hope I should have kept
my

my distance. Ly. Osborne would tell
me that I were growing as careless as
her son, if she saw me in this condition.''
—The Ladies were not wanting in civil
returns ; & Robert Watson stealing a
veiw of his own head in an opposite
glass,—said with equal civility, '' You
cannot be more in dishabille than myself.—We got here so late, that I had
not time even to put a little fresh
powder in my hair.''—Emma could
not help entering into what she sup-
posed her Sister in law's feelings at that
moment.—When the Teathings were
removed, Tom began to talk of his
Carriage—but the old Card Table being
set out, & the fish & counters with a
tolerably clean pack brought forward
from the beaufit by Miss Watson, the
general voice was so urgent with him
to join their party, that he agreed to
allow himself another quarter of an
hour.

hour. Even Emma was pleased that he would stay, for she was beginning to feel that a family party might be the worst of all parties ; & the others were delighted.—" What's your Game ?"— cried he, as they stood round the Table. —" Speculation I beleive, said Elizth— My Sister recommends it, & I fancy we all like it. I know *you* do, Tom."— " It is the only round game played at Croydon now, said Mrs Robert—we never think of any other. I am glad it is a favourite with you."—" Oh ! me ! cried Tom. Whatever you decide on, will be a favourite with *me*.—I have had some pleasant hours at Specula- tion in my time—but I have not been in the way of it now for a long while.— Vingt-un is the game at Osborne Castle ; I have played nothing but Vingt-un of late. You would be astonished to hear the noise we make there.—The

fine

fine old, lofty Drawing-room rings
again. Ly Osborne sometimes declares
she cannot hear herself speak.—Ld.
Osborne enjoys it famously—he makes
the best Dealer without exception that
I ever beheld—such quickness & spirit !
he lets nobody dream over their cards—
I wish you could see him overdraw
himself on both his own cards—it is
worth anything in the World ! ''—
" Dear me !—cried Marg^t why should
not we play at vingt un ?—I think it is
a much better game than Speculation.
I cannot say I am very fond of Speculation." Mrs Robert offered not another
word in support of the game.—She was
quite vanquished, & the fashions of
Osborne-Castle carried it over the
fashions of Croydon.—" Do you see
much of the Parsonage family at the
Castle, Mr Musgrave ?—'' said Emma,
as they were taking their seats.—

" Oh !

" Oh ! yes—they are almost always
there. Mrs Blake is a nice little goodhumoured Woman, she & I are sworn
friends ; & Howard's a very gentlemanlike good sort of fellow !—You are
not forgotten I assure you by any of the
party. I fancy you must have a little
cheek-glowing now & then Miss Emma.
Were not you rather warm last Saturday
about 9 or 10 o'clock in the Even^g—?
I will tell you how it was.—I see you
are dieing to know.—Says Howard
to Ld Osborne—'' At this interesting
moment he was called on by the others,
to regulate the game & determine some
disputable point ; & his attention was
so totally engaged in the business &
afterwards by the course of the game as
never to revert to what he had been
saying before ;—& Emma, tho' suffer-
ing a good deal from Curiosity, dared
not remind him.—He proved a very
useful

useful addition at their Table; without him, it w^d have been a party of such very near relations as could have felt little Interest, & perhaps maintained little complaisance, but his presence gave variety & secured good manners. —He was in fact excellently qualified to shine at a round Game; & few situations made him appear to greater advantage. He played with spirit, & had a great deal to say & tho' with no wit himself, c^d sometimes make use of the wit of an absent friend; & had a lively way of retailing a commonplace, or saying a mere nothing, that had great effect at a Card Table. The ways, & good Jokes of Osborne Castle were now added to his ordinary means of Entertainment; he repeated the smart sayings of one Lady, detailed the oversights of another, & indulged them even with a copy of Ld Osborne's stile of overdrawing

overdrawing himself on both cards.—
The Clock struck nine, while he was
thus agreably occupied; & when
Nanny came in with her Master's
Bason of Gruel, he had the pleasure
of observing to Mr Watson that he
should leave him at supper, while he
went home to dinner himself.—The
Carriage was ordered to the door—&
no entreaties for his staying longer c^d
now avail,—for he well knew, that if
he staid he must sit down to supper
in less than ten minutes—which to a
Man whose heart had been long fixed
on calling his next meal a Dinner, was
quite insupportable.—On finding him
determined to go, Marg^t began to wink
& nod at Elizth to ask him to dinner
for the following day; & Eliz. at last
not able to resist hints, which her own
hospitable, social temper more than half
seconded, gave the invitation. " Would

Q   he

he give Robt the meeting, they sh^d be
very happy." "With the greatest
pleasure"—was his first reply. In a
moment afterwards—" That is if I can
possibly get here in time—but I shoot
with Ld Osborne, & therefore must
not engage—You will not think of
me unless you see me."—And so, he
departed, delighted with the uncer-
tainty in which he had left it.—

Marg^t in the joy of her heart under
circumstances, which she chose to consider as peculiarly propitious, would
willingly have made a confidante of
Emma when they were alone for a short
time the next morn^g; & had proceeded so far as to say—" The young
man who was here last night my dear
Emma & returns today, is more interesting to me, than perhaps you may
be aware—" but Emma pretending to
understand

understand nothing extraordinary in the words, made some very inapplicable reply, & jumping up, ran away from a subject which was odious to her feelings.—

As Marg[t] would not allow a doubt to be repeated of Musgrave's coming to dinner, preparations were made for his Entertainment much exceeding what had been deemed necessary the day before ; and taking the office of superintendance intirely from her sister, she was half the morning in the Kitchen herself directing & scolding.—After a great deal of indifferent Cooking, & anxious Suspense however they were obliged to sit down without their Guest.—T. Musgrave never came, & Marg[t] was at no pains to conceal her vexation under the disappointment, or repress the peevishness of her Temper—. The Peace of the party for the

the remainder of that day, & the whole
of the next, which comprised the
length of Robert & Jane's visit, was
continually invaded by her fretful dis-
pleasure, & querulous attacks.—Eliz.
was the usual object of both. Marg^t
had just respect enough for her B^r &
S^{rs} opinion, to behave properly by
them, but Eliz. & the maids c^d never
do anything right—& Emma, whom
she seemed no longer to think about,
found the continuance of the gentle
voice beyond her calculation short.
Eager to be as little among them as
possible, Emma was delighted with the
alternative of sitting above, with her
father, & warmly entreated to be his
constant Comp^n each Even^g—& as
Eliz. loved company of any kind too
well, not to prefer being below, at all
risks, as she had rather talk of Croydon
to Jane, with every interruption of
Marg$^{t'}$s

Marg^t's perverseness, than sit with only her father, who frequently c^d not endure Talking at all, the affair was so settled, as soon as she could be persuaded to beleive it no sacrifice on her Sister's part.—To Emma, the exchange was most acceptable, & delightful. Her father, if ill, required little more than gentleness & silence ; &, being a Man of Sense & Education, was if able to converse, a welcome companion.—

In *his* chamber, Emma was at peace from the dreadful mortifications of unequal Society, & family Discord—from the immediate endurance of Hardhearted prosperity, low-minded Conceit, & wrong-headed folly, engrafted on an untoward Disposition.—She still suffered from them in the Contemplation of their existence ; in memory & in prospect, but for the moment, she ceased to be tortured by their effects.—

She

She was at leisure, she could read &
think,—tho' her situation was hardly
such as to make reflection very soothing. The Evils arising from the loss of
her Uncle, were neither trifling, nor
likely to lessen ; & when Thought had
been freely indulged, in contrasting the
past & the present, the employment of
mind, the dissipation of unpleasant
ideas which only reading could produce,
made her thankfully turn to a book.—
The change in her home society, & stile
of Life in consequence of the death
of one friend and the imprudence of
another had indeed been striking.—
From being the first object of Hope &
Solicitude to an Uncle who had formed
her mind with the care of a Parent, &
of Tenderness to an Aunt whose ami-
able temper had delighted to give her
every indulgence, from being the Life
& Spirit of a House, where all had been
comfort

comfort & Elegance, & the expected Heiress of an easy Independance, she was become of importance to no one, a burden on those, whose affection she c^d not expect, an addition in an House, already overstocked, surrounded by inferior minds with little chance of domestic comfort, & as little hope of future support.—It was well for her that she was naturally chearful ;—for the Change had been such as might have plunged weak spirits in Despondence.—

She was very much pressed by Robert & Jane to return with them to Croydon, & had some difficulty in getting a refusal accepted ; as they thought too highly of their own kind-ness & situation, to suppose the offer could appear in a less advantageous light to anybody else.—Elizth gave them her interest, tho' evidently against her own, in privately urging Emma to

go

go—" You do not know what you
refuse Emma—said she—nor what you
have to bear at home.—I would advise
you by all means to accept the invitation, there is always something lively
going on at Croydon, you will be in
company almost every day, & Robt &
Jane will be very kind to you.—As for
me, I shall be no worse off without you,
than I have been used to be ; but poor
Marg^{ts} disagreable ways are new to *you*,
& they would vex you more than you
think for, if you stay at home.—"
Emma was of course un-influenced,
except to greater esteem for Elizth, by
such representations—& the Visitors
departed without her.—

From the second edition (1871) of the Memoir, p. 364:

When the author's sister, Cassandra, showed the manuscript of this work to some of her nieces, she also told them something of the intended story ; for with this dear sister—though, I believe, with no one else—Jane seems to have talked freely of any work that she might have in hand. Mr. Watson was soon to die ; and Emma to become dependent for a home on her narrow-minded sister-in-law and brother. She was to decline an offer of marriage from Lord Osborne, and much of the interest of the tale was to arise from Lady Osborne's[1] love for Mr. Howard, and his counter affection for Emma, whom he was finally to marry.

[1] Doubtless a slip for *Miss Osborne*. Lady O. was 'nearly fifty' (p. 38).

NOTES

NOTES

PAGE 1

2. D. *for* L—
   Surry *over* Sus *erased* (*i.e.* Sussex, *see below*,
   note on p. 8)
3. it was *for* was
16. had *erased before* were accustomed
17. dress *added above line*
18. for *erased before* on every

PAGE 2

2. as only two of M[r] W.'s children were at home,
   & one was always necessary (to him *erased*)
   as companion to himself, for he was sickly
   & had lost his wife, one only *for* one only of
   the Family in Stanton Parsonage
8. who was very recently returned to her family
   from the care of an Aunt who had brought
   her up *added above line*
13. & her eldest sister, whose delight in a Ball was
   not lessened by a ten years Enjoyment, had
   some merit in chearfully undertaking (kindly
   undertook *erased* ; *before* kindly *is a word
   erased, not legible*) to drive her & all her finery
   in the old chair to D. on the important morn[g]
   for & Miss Watson drove her & all her finery
   in the old chair to D. on the important
   morning of the Ball ; without being able to
   stay & share the pleasure herself, because her
   Father who was an Invalid could not be left
   to spend the Even[g]
22. it will be *for* you will have

PAGE 3

1. hardly *for* not
3. and I would advise *for* but I would recommend
9. & hav (?) *erased before* if he does
14. & *erased before* there
16. Tom *for* Charles
    ad *erased before* take notice
19. every *for* any

PAGE 4

15. behaving in a particular way to *for* philandering with (*Miss Austen saw that Miss Watson was unlikely to use such a word*)
16. an *added above line before* other

PAGE 5

6. of the name of Purvis a particular friend of Robert's, who used to be with us a great deal. Every body thought it would have been a Match." A sigh accompanied *over* a neighbour—& he to me. Perhaps you may see him tonight. He is married Purvis & he has the Living of Alford about 14 miles off. We were very much attached to each other *erased*
11. would have *erased before* respected
    in silence *for* too much to urge (continue *above line*) the subject further
12. after a short pause went on *over* had pleasure in the communication *erased*
22. gaining *for* getting

PAGE 6

1. soon after *added above line*
16. There is nothing she w^d not do to (be *erased*) get married—she would as good *over* She w^d not deny it herself ; she makes no secret of wishing to marry *erased*

(126)

NOTES

Page 7

2. I wish with all my heart she was well married.
   I declare I had rather have her well-married
   than myself *over* I wish she were well
   married with all my heart ; when once she
   is, she will be a very worthy character—but
   till then *erased*
16. I have lost *over* Penelope is now *erased*
17. it is true *added above line*

Page 8

5. never means anything *for* meant nothing
8. slight her for *for* take notice of
11. Chichester *for* Southampton (*This alteration
    was no doubt consequent on the change from
    Sussex to Surry*)
14. taken a vast *for* had a monstrous
15. about him *added above line*
17. the other day *added above line*
18. of trial *erased after* last time
20. particular *added above line*
    Chichester *for* Southampton
21. nor guess at the *over* you did not suspect
    erased
    that could *erased and restored*
22. from Stanton *for* from home

Page 9

2. had not the *over* should never have *erased*
7. to be able to *for* I wished to
   an immediate *for* a
10. Asthma *for* Gout

Page 11

10. endeavour to *erased before* correct
17. especially *added above line*
19. is a little fretful & perverse *for* has a good
    deal of spirit

20. creature ! she *for* Margaret
22. more *added above line before* seriously

PAGE 12

4. within this twelvemonth *added above line*
9. now *added above line after* Croydon
17. I do not wonder at you *for* & well you may

PAGE 13

7. & I *added above line after* Musgrave
15. & *added above line before* If
16. Passage *for* Tea-room

PAGE 14

6. made no answer *for* was silenced
19. sh^d *for* shall
20. not *added above line after* should
21. home *added above line*

PAGE 15

6. You must have a sweet temper indeed ; *for* What a sweet temper you must have
7. like it *for* so kind
10. I shall never forget the kindness of the proposal. But *erased before* I am not so selfish
11. that comes to *for* to accept it

PAGE 16

4. her partners *for* their names
5. you know they will be all strangers to me *for* do you wish me particularly to observe them
7. Hunter *for* Carr
8. have my fears in *over* am rather afraid of *erased*
10. it is all over with *for* all the worse for
14. not *added above line before* you know
16. Shropshire *for* Devonshire
17. of that nature in Surry *for* in Sussex

19. such delicacy *for* so delicate a nature
20. communication *for* correspondence
21. you & me for the last 14 *for* in for a dozen
22. years ".] years ; *MS.*

Page 17
11. Guilford *for* Dorking

Page 18
9. six *for* four
22. & the White Hart *for* the Town Hall

Page 19
9. heavily *for* stupidly
16. place, if Mr Tomlinson *for* Town, if
18. newly erected (? one *erased*) House *for* new House
19. with a Shrubbery & sweep *added above line*
20. which however was not often granted *erased after* Country
   was higher than most of its neighbours with two windows on each side the door, (& five *erased*) the windows guarded by (a chain & green *erased*) posts & chain the door approached *over* was of a dull brick colour, & an high Elevation, a flight of stone steps to the Door, & two windows flight of stone steps with white posts, & a chain, divided *erased*

Page 20
9. nice *over* prett *erased*
11. & *added before* They
   I assure you *erased after* stile
13. with *for* & *after* Livery
20. thought *for* idea
21. to *over* fo *erased*
22. too *over* had *erased*
   giving *for* given

2955.4   S

Page 21

1. some very *for* many
   with respect to her own family, had (*originally
   &*) made her more open to (any *and* other
   erased) disagreable impressions from any
   other cause, & increased her sense of the
   awkwardness of rushing into Intimacy on so
   slight an acquaintance] *The corrections here
   are confused ; the following words are erased* :
   to add to the awkwardness of so slight an
   acquaintance to the consciousness of & in
   particular to the awkwardness   *the words*
   seemed a serious Evil   *are also erased after*
   acquaintance
9. change *for* dissipation
10. tho' a very freindly woman, had a reserved air
    for was a very freindly woman, but of rather
    formal aspect
11. & a great *over & erased*
13. a *for* the
    of 22 *added above line*
14. very naturally *for* as was natural
17. Emma *for* She

Page 22

3. & *added above line after* easier,
5. came *for* entered
13. by 9 *for* at 8
15. our Assemblies *for* the Ball
19. more than they deserve *for* not very reason-
    able

Page 23

1. have always their charm *for* must always be
   the vogue, & Little ones love to be infatuated
   by (are very fond of looking at   *above line*)
   them
16. shew *for* appearance
20. respectably *for* safely

PAGE 24

6. of *added above line after* approve
15. gently *over* obs *erased*

PAGE 25

4. his *over* to compare a young Lady to a Man
   whose *erased*
5. has been rather too *for* is pretty
9. had not thought *for* did not think
   degree of *erased before* Likeness
16. 7 *for* ten
17. & if you do not tell me that he is plain there-
    fore (but let him be ever so plain, I have you
    know, I have no right to refuse *above line*)
    being like him *erased before* but my father
20. Yʳ brother's *for* his
22. He has a long (*originally* broad) face, & a wide
    mouth *for* & every feature is different

PAGE 26

10. very strongly (*originally* a strong one) *over* it
    is very strong *erased*
11. I am not sensible of the (*originally* any ?)
    others. (I cannot see any other *erased*) *over*
    for the life of me I cannot any of the others
    that you fancy *erased*
12. I do not much think she is like *for* No—I am
    sure there is no likeness between her, &
19. poured *erased before* helped
20. drawn round the fire to enjoy *for* set in for
22. to *added above line after* drink

PAGE 27

4. does *for* is
   very *added above line before* few
5. better *erased before* fairer
7. For now (*originally* Now) *added above line*
   before We
11. how much he wᵈ enjoy it *for* I think he wᵈ
    enjoy it very much

Page 28

2. calmly *for* gravely
3. The Osbornes are to be no rule for us   *added above line*
4. better *added above line*
5. two hours sooner *over* your party at ten, than *erased*
7. so wise as *for* wise enough
8. & *for* — *after* point ;
9. now *added above line before* turned
10. long enough *for* sufficiently long
12. having *for* he had
13. Circumstances of his young Guest *for* marriage of that (the *above line*) Aunt with whom his young Guest had been used to reside
15. began with *for* observed to her
16. very well *added above line*
17. I am *over* one of the *erased*
18. in the old *for* at Wiltshire's

Page 29

4. " Mr Turner had not been dead a great while I think ? " About 2 years Sir." " I forget what her name is now ? " *over* Mr Her name was Turner—I forget what it is now *erased*
20. drawing up *erased before* the Gentleman

Page 30

4. gravely *added above line*
6. had just *added above line*
   just *erased after* perturbation
8. in remembering *for* to remember
13. choice *for* match
14. Carefulness—Discretion— *for* The Caution
16. choice (marriage *erased*) *over* connection *erased*
18. choice *erased after* first
19. replied he *added above line*

PAGE 31

17. to *erased before* going
19. to *erased before* almost
    wished for *for* desirable

PAGE 32

1. to order *for* ordering
3. & *erased before* warmth
7. while she attended with *over* & watching over
    the *erased*
12. tuning *erased before* Scrape
16. yet *added above line after* people, *erased, and
    restored after* come
    only *erased before* told
17. as she knew she should *added above line after*
    told, *erased, and restored above line after*
    Waiter
21. in (Candle- *erased*) lights *added above line after*
    brilliant
    with Candles *erased after* before them
22. a morning dress & *added above line*

PAGE 33

2. apparently *for* seemingly
6. familiarity *erased before* air
7. The Candles are but this moment lit "—(& I
    am waiting *erased*) " I like to get a good seat
    by the fire you know, Mr Musgrave." replied
    Mrs E. *over* We shall have an a famous Ball.
    —The Osbornes are certainly coming, I can
    answer for that (assure you *above line*) ;
    I was with Ld Osborne this morn^g— *erased*
19. to the fireplace at the upper end *added above
    line*
21. while *over* & a *erased*
    were *added above line before* lounging
22. together *over* about, & *erased*
    backwards & forwards *added over* in & out
    and erased

(133)

PAGE 34

4. placed *for* seated
5. low *for* quiet
6. said *altered to* observed *and restored*
8. then *for* was it *after* Musgrave
19. appearance *for* air
20. & the (solemn *erased*) demure air *over* began
    soon to *erased*
21. at one end of it *added above line*
22. soon *for* now
    way *for* away

PAGE 35

4. giggling *added above line before* girls *and erased*
5. gentleman straggler *for* straggling Man
6. with any fair She (creature *above line*) *erased
    after* Love
7. any fair Creature *for* her
16. rather distressed, but by no means (*originally
    perhaps* but not) *for* rather shy than
19. her Brother Sam's a hopeless case *for* ill
    (poorly *above line*) of her Brother's chances

PAGE 36

3. party *added above line*
4. for beginning *erased after* given
6. which seemed to call the young Men to their
    duty, & people the centre of the room *over*
    & the young to put all the young people in
    motion *erased*
11. middle *for* middling
15. glowing—; (and she had *erased*) which with
    a lively Eye *over* brightened with a fine
    colour *erased*
17. gave *for* she had
18. engage *erased before* make
    that beauty improve *for* it seem greater
20. Even⁸ *for* Ball

NOTES

PAGE 37

3. not quite *for* nearly
20. a *for* his *before* widow-sister
22. had *erased before* probably

PAGE 38

1. imprisoned within his own room, had *added above line*
8. had made a *over* were (*word illegible*) *erased*
13. chiefly *over* her eyes *erased*
17. had by *for* was the
19. all the Dignity *for* quite the air of a Woman
21. Coldness, of *added above line*

PAGE 39

4. for him *added above line*
5. Borough *for* Town
6. he *added above line before* never
7. an *for* a very *before* agreable-looking
8. a *added above line before* little
17. be surprised *for* wonder
20. her *added above line after* near

PAGE 40

3. engaged *added above line*
8. lively *for* fluent
9. soon afterwards *for* after a short time
15. to you *erased after* engagement
20. she *added above line before* turned
22. begin the set *for* the top of the room

PAGE 41

1. in it's happiness *erased after* interesting *and added above line*
3. under *for* in
7. mortification *for* angry feelings
9. second *for* secondary
18. holding out her hand *added above line*

20. in one moment restored to *over* was again all
   (? made as) *erased*
21. looked joyfully at his Mother and (*originally*
   but) (instantly *erased*) stepping forwards
   with an honest (& *inserted*, simple *added
   above line*) Thank you (Maam *inserted*) was instantly ready *over* wanted no farther solicita-
   tion ; & with a Thank you, as honest as his
   smiles, held out his hand in a hurry to *erased*

PAGE 42

3. Thankfulness *for* gratitude
4. look, most expressive *over* truly gratified look
   erased
5. Astonishment *erased before* unexpected
6. & *over* she of (*i.e.* offered ?) *erased*
   Gratitude *for* Thankfulness
8. of *for* for
10. great *erased before* perfect
   could assure her *for* assured M^{rs} B.
16. nearly *added above line before* equal

PAGE 43

2. the happy *added above line*
5. she perceived *erased after* gave her
   inquisitive *added above line*
6. after a time *added above line*
7. under pretence of talking to Charles, stood to
   look (*originally* looking) at his (*originally*
   her) partner *for* spoke to her partner for the
   sake of looking at her
13. continually making opportunities *for* continually taking every opportunity
14. more than civilly, of warmly *erased before*
   addressing
21. & their Mama *added above line*

PAGE 44

3. & *added above line before* that
4. already *added above line*

11. close to her *for* within a yard (veiw *above line*) of her
13. her *for* the *before* proper
14. always *erased after* company *and added above line before* the pleasure
16. refreshment *over* what nine out of ten had no inclination *erased*
17. The Tearoom was a small room within the Cardroom *added above line*
19. latter, where *for* Cardroom where *erased*
21. hemmed in *for* unable to proceed
22. It happened *for* Emma saw herself

PAGE 45

1. Mr Howard who belonged to it *over* & saw at the same time *erased*
3. herself the object of attention (to *erased*) both to Ly. O. & him *over* that both Lady & Gentleman were *erased*
6. to avoid seeming to hear *for* when she heard
7. companion *for* partner
8. aloud *for* in a very audible voice
   to his Uncle (Mr H *above line*) *erased before* Oh !
9. To her great relief *added above line after* pretty ! *and erased*
10. As *added before* They
11. however *for* &
    was hurried off (from *erased*) *over* left his Uncle *erased*
15. prepared *for* set out
16. quite alone *for* seated
    as if retreating as far as he could from the *over* away from every body else, as if to enjoy his own Thoughts *erased*
21. he cried *erased after* Osborne
22. " No, no, (said Emma laughing *added above line*) you must sit with my (party *erased*)

friends " *over* (But To this *above line*)
Emma could not quite agree to this *erased*
The following passage is completely erased :
& Charles at any rate very happy, was con-
tented (easily overruled *above line*) to sit
where she chose ; and she (& when she soon
afterwards *above line*) saw Ld Osborne so
soon afterwards driven away by the approach
of others (a party *above line*) that *followed by*
She did not fail to remark (*originally* observe)
(*word illegible above line*) that (how very un-
welcome *above line*) they should probably
have been very little welcome themselves
over she c^d not imagine the companionable-
ness of either Charles or herself would have
given his Ld:ship much (were at all to his
taste *above line*).

PAGE 46

5. almost *erased before* Eleven
11. she *for* Emma *before* felt
12. no better reason to give than that Miss Osborne's (*sic*) had *not* kept *for* nothing to
guide her beleif, but Miss Osborne's having
broken

PAGE 47

1. Tea *for* the Tea Tables
was *for* were
3. which happened to be *for* & it was
4. one or two *for* some
5. just *added above line before* broken
6. the players *for* their members
move *for* come
9. were they within reach of Emma *for* had they
met
12. my dear *added above line*
20. in opposite directions *for* different ways

NOTES

PAGE 48

2. suited her *over* she liked greatly approved *erased*
4. increased *for* rose
5. in the Cardroom *added above line*
7. with Tom Musgrave *erased after* lounging
8. say *erased before* call
   Tom *added above line*
9. Why do not you *over* Musgrave, when *erased*
10. that beautiful *added above line*
11. her *for* that girl
12. She is a beautiful Creature *erased after* by you
13. determining (on it *inserted*) this *over* thinking of being *erased*
    to be introduced to her *erased after* moment
14. I'll be introduced *added above line*
17. to *added above line after* Talking
21. her *added above line after* find

PAGE 49

3. exactly the (directly *erased*) *over* into the *erased*

PAGE 50

8. beleive *for* suppose
9. with *for* by
16. She *for* who *after* Mrs E.
20. a little *for* quite

PAGE 51

4. with some amusement perceived *for* saw with some amusement
5. soon soon *erased before* began
   make civil enquiries *for* enquire
11. this neglect *for* their absence
13. Miss Watson the only *over* said Emma with civil *erased*
20. & I confess *added above line before* It
22. I shall *now* endeavour to *for* I feel that I shall soon

(139)

PAGE 52

2. to all this gallantry *erased after* reply
3. gratitude of her sisters *erased before* encouraging
8. bestowed *for* gave
9. being *for* was *after* Carr
12. on seeing Mr Howard come forward & claim Emma's hand *for* by seeing Howard come to claim his partner
15. when his friend carried him the news *for* when answering his friend's communication
18. two *added above line before* dances
20. to Emma *erased after* engagement

PAGE 53

2. topics *over* matt (?) *erased*
   a sensible *for* an easy
3. way *over* & unpretending manner which *erased*
11. the Osborne (*sic*) & their Train *for* the Osborne Party
13. Musgrave *erased after* Tom
16. quite *added above line before* enough
17. I assure you *added above line*
18. shew myself *over* (out *above line*) stay your party *erased*
19. Ly. Osborne *for* Miss Osborne
20. her Carriage *for* the Carriage
   retreat *for* retire
22. the most remote (corner of *above line*, room in *erased*) the House (*originally* Inn), where I shall *over* my own room, where I have ordered *erased*

PAGE 54

3. if you can *erased after* word
4. she *for* Emma Watson
7. at least *added above line*
9. like *for* of *before* a jerking

11. even *added above line before* Ly. Osborne
12. actually *added above line*
14. f *erased after* look
15. the gloves *for* his gloves
16. at the same moment *erased after* compressed

PAGE 55

1. Bar *for* little parlour
2. D *erased before* happy
4. some respects unpleasantly *over* such various ways, so much *erased*
12. Edwards's *erased before* Dining room
13. where the Table was prepared, (for Supper *erased*), & the neat *over* where the cloth was (neat *above line*) *erased*
16. at an end *for* over
17. A great deal of kind pleasure was expressed *for* They all expressed their pleasure
20. as warm as herself, in praise of the fullness, brilliancy *over* particularly earnest in praising the excellence of the Meeting *erased*

PAGE 56

1. the same *for* one
4. scarcely perceived *over* of little concern known to him *erased*
5. 4 *for* 5 *before* rubbers
13. " I was always engaged when they asked me " *added above line*
18. I had heard you say *for* you had told me
22. I thought it had been for the *over* till Capt. Hunter assured me *erased*

PAGE 57

7. was repeated, in a very humble tone *added above line*
12. a Cousin *over* freind *erased*
13. " And who is Mr Styles ? " " One of his particular freinds " *for* & Mr Styles is one of his particular freinds "

PAGE 58

2. their engaging themselves *for* Engagements
13. way of the *added above line before* place
14. on *added above line before* the morn^g
16. now *added above line before* increased *and erased*
    in the present instance *added above line*
18. on Emma's account, as *over* to see the girl who *erased*

PAGE 59

5. grace, & others could *over* thing good looking wh (?) *erased*
12. by finding *for* to find
    & considering that she had heard *over* and no Chair come for *erased*
14. After this discovery she had walked twice to the window ᵗo examine the Street, & *for* Twice had she ⸱alked to the window to look for it—& she
22. but *for* tho' *after* convenient

PAGE 60

1. Family Equipage (too long ? *erased*) perceived *over* conveyance she expected *erased*
2. Mr Musgrave was shortly afterwards announced *for* In two minutes Mr Musgrave entered the room
4. her very stiffest look *for* a stiffer look than usual
5. however *added above line after* dismayed *and erased after* air
6. paid *for* made (?)
11. But to which] *the passage is obscure.* But to which he *may originally have been* But which
12. observe (*small word erased, not legible*) that a verbal postscript *is written over* must (added, will not comment *erased*)

(142)

16. to use no ceremony *for* not to stand on any ceremony
22. his Road lay (*over* he had therefore ta [taken] *erased*) quite (*originally* a) wide from R. *over* different way *erased*

PAGE 61

1. come *for* be fetched
15. at that moment *added above line*
17. Errand *for* Embassy

PAGE 62

2. bring *for* have
6. terms *for* any degree
7. fearful of encroaching on the *for* without assistance from the
8. as well as wishing to go home *over* she could not avoid going home *erased*
10. what *originally* hi[s]
21. afraid *for* fearful

PAGE 63

6. if *added above line before* you can not
7. do so *for* do it
11. longed *for* wished
& she accepted the offer most (very *erased*) thankfully ; acknowledging that as Eliz: was entirely alone *for* but without at all expecting—Eliz: being quite alone,
22. none of them the smallest *for* no

PAGE 65

3. vacancy anywhere *for* room for anybody more
5. Emma said this *for* said Emma
6. against *added above line*
16. Fanny *for* Miss
18. piquante ; & What *for* piquante ;——What
20. That *added above line before* He
21. even, tho' *for* if

(143)

Page 66

18. it was Dinner hour at Stanton *for* Eliz: was just sitting down to dinner
21. Miss W. *for* Eliz:

Page 67

12. the next day *for* on friday or Saturday
13. & was not detained to wait (soon sent away *above line*) *erased after* dinner
14. continued Eliz: *added above line*
20. the use of his Carriage *for* his bringing me home
22. even *added above line before* have liked

Page 68

8. clever *for* nice
9. Besides *for* &
19. Mary *for* her (*italic*)

Page 69

4. perhaps (solely *originally* only *erased*) merely *over* most likely *erased*
6. come to her knowledge *for* reached her
7. Yes *added above line after* dear
8. heard *originally* had
9. Poor Sam !—(It *erased*) He *over* Yes, she knows (very *added above line*) well *erased*
19. Why *added above line over* He
20. is not he ? *erased after* Grand ones

Page 70

5. set *added above line after* Osborne's
14. On the contrary, he seems *for* He is
16. absolutely *added above line*
20. company *added above line*
21. (emotion *erased*) other (*originally* than) agreable Emotion *over* other pleasure *erased*

PAGE 71

1. It is well Margaret (w *erased*) is not by.—You do not offend *me*, tho' I hardly know *over* Do not let Margaret hear such words ; (that's all *above line*) she would never forgive you
17. ; & *for* — *before* spread

PAGE 72

1. very *erased before* proud
2. can speak as you do, of *for* are not infatuated by
3. my heart did misgive *for* for my heart misgave
8. & that he will not come on *for* But if he should come
22. everybody were *over* poor Marg^t loved *erased*

PAGE 73

2. say *erased before* owns
17. continued Mr W. *added above line*
19. & in a very (*originally* an) impressive manner *added above line*
22. own, I do not like *for* have an abhorrence of

PAGE 74

1. I do not like (I cannot endure *erased*) the *over* *and under* & of the *erased*
2. artificial *added above line*
16. & seemed to feel *over* as an Invalid *erased*

PAGE 75

3. is *for* are *before* a pretty
5. quite *added above line before* agree
6. walked by me from the bottom to the top, & would *added above line for* would *erased*
11. I never *over* except *erased*
17. at *added above line before* five
   the dinner hour at Stanton *erased after* three
19. she was suddenly called to *over* two gentle-men on Horseback *erased*

Page 76

1. tho' charged by Miss W. to let nobody in, re: *over* after a short exercise of wonder and curiosity (pause of curiosity on the part *above line*) of the Miss Watsons, they were *erased*
3. awkward *added above line before* dismay
4. parlour *added above line before* door
8. a *added above line before* moment
9. as these *over* were *erased*
13. on *for* after
22. & having *added above line before* In she had *erased after* family

Page 77

2. was *over* & *erased after* Life she had not quite philosophy enough to be (she could not without some mortification consider *above line*) *erased before* fully sensible
4. Of *for* From
5. knew very little *for* was free
7. and tho' shrinking under a general Sense of Inferiority, (she *added above line*) felt no (peculiar *erased*) particular *over* & she wished (*words illegible, perhaps* them away), more from a sense of Convenience than of Shame *erased before* Shame
10. the Gentlemen *for* they
12. the gentlemen *erased before* With (*originally* with)
13. they *added above line before* took
20. not caught *for* taken no
21. time *for* minutes

Page 78

1. fair *added above line before* neighbour
5. remark *for* question
13. looks very well *for* have a very good air

16. lo [lose ?] *deleted before* injure
    are not fit for *for* have not (*originally* no)
    advantage in the deep dirt of
20. ride *erased after* does not

PAGE 79

6. Your Lordship] *This passage, as far as* rewarded by a (page 80, line 13) *is written on a
   separate piece of paper, f. 30 ª ; for the passage
   which it replaced, see the end of these notes.*
13. will *for* may *after* Economy
    my Lord *added above line after* deal
18. it's mild seriousness, as well as in the words
    themselves *for* what she said
22. a degree of considerate *for* courteous

PAGE 80

3. It was a new thing with him to wish to please
   a woman ; it was the first time that he had
   ever felt *over* You have not been long in
   this Country I understand.—I hope you are
   pleased with its—the delicate *erased*
6. in Emma's situation *for* his equal in Education
9. effect *for* resolving on the necessary effort
11. in the tone of a Gentle^{n} *added above line*
14. full *added above line before* veiw
15. on him *erased after* bestowed
17. then *added above line before* sat
18. some *for* about five
21. half *over* putting *erased*

PAGE 81

3. hitherto *added above line*
6. called (loudly *erased*) briskly *over* was calling
   erased
9. goodhumouredly *added above line*
11. you *added above line before* know

15. Ld Osborne's parting Comp^{ts} took some time *for* Ld Osborne took some time to pay his parting Comp^{ts} to Emma
16. his inclination for speech] the *and* his readiness at words *are erased*
21. begged that his Sister might be allow'd to send Emma *for* wanted her to allow his Sister to send her

2. My Hounds will *for* I shall
5. at 9 o'clock *added above line* I mention this, in hopes of y^r being *for* I hope you will be
7. going on] *After these words the following are erased :* Nobody can be indifferent to the glorious sounds (Everybody allows that there is not so fine a sight in the world *above line*) as a pack of Hounds (a pack of Fox- *above line*) in full cry. I am sure you will be pleased (delighted *above line*) to hear the first Burst —if we can (but *above line*) find there as I dare say we shall.
8. pray do us the honour of giving us your good wishes in person *for* do not be kept at home
15. Stanton] *After this word the following are erased :* I wish he would give my poor Father a Living, as he makes such a point of coming to see him. But (to be sure *above line*) Mr Howard will have every thing he has to give (of that kind sort *above line*) (Ld O. is very *erased*) He is very *over* He has a *erased*
16. young Man *erased after* handsome
17. smartest & *added above line*
18. Man *erased and restored*
20. w^d not have had *for* should not have liked

talk to such a great Man for the world *for* to have had to speak to him
22. But *added above line before* Did

PAGE 83

1. him ask *over* leave (?) her *erased*
3. It *for* He *before* put
6. just *erased and restored before* the Tray
11. was *repeated by accident and erased before* by no means
12. His coming (of (?) *erased*) was a sort of notice which might please her vanity, but (c^d not be welcome to *erased*) did not suit her pride *for* for the sort of notice though agreable (welcome *above line*) to her vanity, was not soothing to her pride *all erased*
18. feelings *for* reflections
19. had *erased before* once
20. why *for* that

PAGE 84

2. that *erased before* had declined
3. carried *for* had
4. in it's form as Goodbreeding *for* as Goodbreeding in it
5. M^r W was very far from being delighted, when he *over* When Mr Watson *erased*
7. a little *over* he expressed no *erased*
8. ill disposed *for* indisposed
9. replied *for* said
11. Ld O.'s coming *for* it
12. 14 *for* twelve
13. It *for* This *before* is some foolery
15. *I added above line before* would
19. too-sufficient *for* too-reasonable
20. infirm *for* infirmiti
22. after this visit *over* after this visit, at Stanton Parsonage *erased*

PAGE 85

3. mutual regard *for* regard for each other
5. of each other *added above line after* knowledge
7. in *added above line after* break
12. & wished to see their Sister Emma *added above line*
15. hom *erased before* Stanton
    busy *for* employ
    (time *erased*) hours *over* Corporeal powers *erased*
21. she *added above line before* could make

PAGE 86

1. An absence of 14 years had made all her Brothers & Sisters *over* Emma had not heard any thing of Margaret to make *erased*
6. heard *added above line before* things
9. almost *added above line before* all that
13. & *erased before* very well satisfied
15. Attorney *for* Man
21. as *erased before* genteel

PAGE 87

6. but the sharp & anxious *over* the *erased*
7. made her beauty *over* sharp & anxious *erased*
9. long-absent *added above line*
10. manner was all *over* smiles were very *erased*
12. (distinguished her *erased*) being her constant *over* were her constant *erased*
13. resource *over* were what she (had *above line*) always recoursed to
16. she could hardly speak a word in a minute *for* the words seemed likely never to end
21. a proposition—& *over* an observation *erased*

PAGE 88

5. at the moment of meeting *for* & in her husband's on meeting her
6. & she cd. not but feel how much better it was

to be the daughter of a gentleman of (easy *erased*) *over* they had not been ten minutes together before the latter shewed that it was *erased*

10. threw herself away on *for* gave all her money to

11. Captain *for* officer

14. Post-Boy *over* Postboy Driver *erased*

15. advance *for* rise

PAGE 89

1. Surveyor *for* Overseer

2–19. neice *for* nephew, Augusta *for* John, *and* her *for* him *or* his

8. very *added above line before* hard

10. say we were only going to Church & promise *over* send him out a-walking, & promise not *erased*

14. as particular as ever *for* very particular

18. Then *added above line before* Why

22. as (?) *erased after* Such

PAGE 90

3. if it be *added above line*

4. & *added above line before* I am sorry she added *erased after* sorry we have not been able to make Croydon agreable *for* you have found Croydon so disagreable

9. spare me, I entreat you *over* but *erased*

21. seven *for* nine *before* Tables

22. Drawingroom *for* two Drawingrooms

PAGE 91

6. indeed *added above line before* wondering

7. home Emma *for* place she

8. possibly *added above line before* have been used to

16. (5 minutes afterwards *erased*) when she heard
    Marg^t 5 minutes afterwards say *over* on
    overhearing Marg^t saying *erased*
18. accent *for* tone
19. lately *erased before* since
    to Chichester *for* away

PAGE 92

21. now *added above line before* I do hope

PAGE 93

2. rather quickly *added above line*
6. & *for* — *before* rather mortified
13. on entering it *added above line*
14. there *erased after* brother
21. said *for* thought
22. as soon as her Husband died *for* when she
    took you away

PAGE 94

2. smiling *erased after* Emma
4. placed *written above* secured *and erased*
   your *for* you after
   in Trust *erased after* use
8. being (probable *above line*) *erased before*
   Heiress
11. Do not *for* I beg you not to
12. her *for* my Aunt, Brother
13. & *for* — *before* If
18. I thought Turner] *This passage, as far as* he
    added (page 96, line 13) *is written on a
    separate piece of paper, f. 35* ^a.
21. leave *erased before* make

PAGE 95

5. for me *erased after* unfortunate
6. if possible *added above line*
11. every thing that he had to dispose of, or any
    part of it *for* it all

(152   )

16. herself *for* her
20. & *added above line before* without

PAGE 96

1. such a *over* 14 years *erased*
3. among us *added above line*
22. man *added above line*

PAGE 97

4. Robert, who had equally (mortified, *erased*)
    irritated & greived her *over* her brother
    erased
19. tho' *for* if
21. too (?) *erased after* gentlemen

PAGE 98

4. pu *erased before* wear it (*Miss Austen intended*
    put, *but avoided the repetition*)
9. tho' in no Spirits to make such nonsense easy
    added above line
14. excessively *for* very much
22. on *for* of *before* the Table

PAGE 99

1. the entrance of *over* having *erased, and*
    brought in *erased after* dinner "
11. as *for* & *before* stay
12. Besides *added above line before* If
    in *added above line before* hopes

PAGE 100

6. help *erased before* break
21. why do not you *for* but you must
22. at *added above line before* Cribbage

PAGE 101

1. always *erased before* played
4. caught *for* heard
5. it became *for* & it grew

NOTES

9. very *added above line before* public
11. in two minutes *added above line*
17. creature to be *over* person *erased*
18. She *over* as tolerably likely *erased*
19. unexpected *for* sudden
20. Steps were distinguished, first along the paved *for* Footsteps were heard ascending (upon *added above line and erased*) the paved (gravel *added above line and erased*)
22. led *for* lead

PAGE 102

1. from the gate *erased before* front door
2. within *for* in
5. displayed *for* shewed
6. in *for* — *before* the wrap
13. he *erased after* instance
18. however *added above line*
19. give *for* create
21. little *added above line before* sitting room
22. a foot larger each way than the other *added above line*

PAGE 103

2. he *added above line before* beheld
4. *before* arranged *a word is erased which is perhaps* sollem (*i.e.* sollemnly)
7. with *over* making *erased*
8. stood *for* stopt, for
12. such *over* himself *erased*
19. who closed (*sic*) observed him, perceived nothing that did not justify Eliz'ˢ opinions *over* discerned no more than she had expected, tho *erased*

PAGE 104

4. For *added above line before* Whether
5. as *added above line before* he observed
6. and (took *erased*) without seeming to seek, he

did not (avoid *erased*) turn away from the chair close to *over* He did not seem to avoid the seat by *erased*

10. thus *added above line before* secured
15. ago *for* back
17. understood *for* enquired into
18. let *over* yeild *erased*
19. & (or ? *erased*) important demands *over* more domestic enquiries *erased*
22. spoke her fears of his having *for* feared he must have

Page 105

6. Horse Guards *added above* Bedford *but erased* of Lord Osbornes *erased after* friend
9. Ho (*or* It ?) *erased before* We very *erased before* morn^g

Page 106

1. what are my Sensations *over* how great my enjoyment *erased*
2. in the bosom of my Family *erased after* Stanton
12. " Oh ! you Creature ! "—was Margaret's reply *erased after* finish
17. at this moment *for* likewise

Page 107

9. a dark complexion can *over* the hue of her ski *erased*
12. my model for a truly *over* very fair, Miss Osborne *erased*
14. Is she fairer than me ? *for* She is about as fair as I am, I think
15. Tom made no reply.—" Upon my *over* Instead of making any reply, Tom *erased*
18. highly endebted to your *over* most fervently ashamed *erased*
20. Dishabille *for* a state

NOTES

21. unfit *replaced by* unsuitably *and restored*
22. to be here *for* to for your presence *erased*

PAGE 108

5. & *for* — *before* Robert
    stealing *for* took *erased*
6. slight *erased before* veiw
7. said *over* and he *erased*
    said *erased after* civility
10. fresh *added above line before* powder
13. at that moment *for* must be on this occasion
16. old *added above line before* Card
    being set out, & *over* was placed *erased*
17. with *for* & *before* a tolerably
19. from the beaufit *added above line*
21. agreed to *for* would

PAGE 109

1. in their *erased after* hour
3. party *replaced by* circle *and restored*
4. & *added above line before* the others
16. enough *erased after* hours
17. played at *erased before* been in the way

PAGE 110

4. famously *for* amazingly
    — *for* & *before* he makes
5. without exception that I ever beheld *for* in
    the world
6. spirit ! he lets *for* spirit ;—lets
7. their cards *for* it
8. overdraw himself *over* deal himself *erased*
9. his own *added above line before* cards
13. a *added above line before* much better
15. offered *over* withdrew *and* said *both erased*
16. She was quite vanquished, & the (Croydon
    erased) fashions of Osborne- *over* Osborne
    Castle carried it, even in her estimation *erased*

(156)

19. the fashions *for* those
    after fashions of Croydon *follows :*
    T. Musgrave was a very (most *above line*) use-
    ful addition ; without him, it would have
    been a
    These words are deleted and the inserted pas-
    sage f. 40ª (Do you see much *to* page 112
    line 2, have been a) *pinned over them*
22. as *for* while *after* Emma

PAGE 111

1. they are *added above line before* almost
3. gr *erased after* sworn
6. the party *for* them
8. Miss Emma *added above line*
12. Howard to Lᵈ Osborne *for* Lᵈ Osborne to
    Howard
14. called on *for* interrupted
17. & afterwards by the course of the game *added*
    above line
20. could not remind him *erased after* Emma
21. dared *for* could
22. He proved] *for the original version of this*
    sentence see the note on page 110 l. 19 above

PAGE 112

1. at *for* to *before* their Table
3. could *over* w (?) *erased* ; must *added above,*
    but erased
    felt little *for* deadened the
4. maintained little *for* even impaired the
5. of the players *erased after* complaisance
7. in fact *added above line*
8. & (seldom *erased*) few situations made him
    appear *for* he never appeared
10. He played with spirit, & had a great deal to
    say (He played with Eagerness *erased*) *over*
    than when assisting at one, & He talked
    much *erased*

11. with no wit himself, c^d sometimes *over* without wit, sometimes said a lively thing *erased*
14. saying *erased before* retailing
15. (did *erased*) had great effect *over* was abundantly useful *erased*
18. ordinary *added above line*
20. one Lady *for* Miss Osborne
21. another *for* Miss Carr
even *added above line*
22. stile *originally* m

Page 113

2. while *for* as
11. avail *for* prevail
for he well knew, that if he staid *for* if he staid, he knew
13. less than *added above line*
14. must (?) *erased before* heart *and* who *corrected to* whose
had been long *for* was
15. calling his next meal a Dinner *for* a very late dinner
was quite (must be *erased*) *over* was *erased*
17. to go *added above line*
20. hints, which her own *over* & from her *erased*
21. more than half seconded *over* not above half wishing *erased*

Page 114

4. That is *added above line*
5. here *for* home
6. must not engage *for* cannot positively answer
7. You will not think of *over* & In another moment *erased*
10. left *for* placed
16. & *for* — *before* proceeded

Page 115

3. ran away *for* made her escape
7. repeated *for* entertained

10. done *erased before* deemed
11. f *erased before* before
   for Mrs Robert *erased after* before
   taking the office of superintendance intirely
   from her Sister (for the occasion *erased*) she
   over superseding all Eliz.'s cares usual cares,
   she (*word illegible above line*) *erased*
14. herself *added above line*
15. indifferent Cooking, & anxious Suspense however *over* Cooking, & waiting (*or possibly*
   wasting) *erased*
20. under the disappointment, or *over* or *erased*

PAGE 116

5. attacks *for* altercations
6. Marg^t *for* She
10. whom *over* found the *erased*
12. continuance of the *for* affec^te (*i.e.* affectionate)
   (even shorter lived *erased*) beyond her calculation (breif *erased*) short *over* more short
   lived even than she had expected *erased*
14. Eager (Glad *erased*) *for* Delighted
15. Emma was delighted with the alternative of
   sitting (upstairs *erased*) above *is substituted
   for the following passage, partly illegible and
   several times corrected :* Emma was glad to
   (*for* eager to ; constant (?) *added above line*)
   prefer (?) & invita (?) sitting with (*erasure
   above line*) in attending her Father who *over*
   take Eliz.'s usual place (with *erased*) in their
   Father's room *all heavily erased*
17. & warmly entreated to be his constant Comp^n
   each Even^g *for* who was confined both days
   to his room
18. as Eliz. *for* Eliz. who
20. (when *erased*) at all risks *over* while she c^d be
   (leive *erased ?*) persuaded to beleive it no
   sacrifice on Emma's part *erased*

21. as *added above line before* She had rather
22. to *for* with *after* Croydon
    every interruption *for* all the interruptions

PAGE 117

3. the affair was *for* it was soon
6. the exchange was most acceptable, & delight-
    ful *for* it was a most acceptable, & delightful
    releif
8. little more than *for* only
9. &, being a Man of Sense & Education, was if
    able to converse, a welcome *over* if able to
    converse, as he was (being *above line*) a man
    of Education & Taste, he was a pleasing
    erased
13. mortifications *for* Evils
16. low-minded Conceit (and a *erased*) *over* mean
    spirited Self-sufficiency *erased*
17. folly, engrafted *over* ill disposed *erased*
18. still *added above line before* suffered
19. in the Contemplation *over* only in *erased*
22. ceased to be *over* she had a pause *erased*
    effects *for* effusions

PAGE 118

1. was *over* could *erased*
2. tho' her *for* Her
    perhaps *added above line after* situation *and
    erased*
    hardly *for* not
4. Evils arising from the loss of her Uncle *for*
    misfortunes which her Uncle's death had
    brought on her
5. neither *over* every day *erased*
7. in contrasting the past & the present *for* when
    the past & the present had been contrasted
8. the dissipations *erased before* the employment
10. reading *altered to* Books *and restored*
11. a book *for* them

12. The sink (fall *above line*) in her fortunes, the *erased before* The (*above line*) change & *added above line before* stile
13. had *erased after* Life
    the death of one friend (Mrs Turner's *above line*) & the *over* her Aunt's *erased*
14. of another, had indeed been materialy (*the last word is doubtful*) *added above line after* imprudence *and erased*
    (the infatuation *erased*) of another had indeed been striking *over* had been great & greivous *erased*
22. whole *erased before* House

2. Inh *erased before* Heiress
3. become of importance *over* reduced to a House *erased*
4. those, whose affection she c^d not expect, an addition in an House, already overstocked, surrounded by inferior minds with *over* an already too full House, where she was felt as an Intruder, a Stranger among those *erased*
8. enjo *erased before* comfort
   as little hope of *for* no hope of a
10. for the Change had been such as (to *erased*) might have plunged *over* as (?) it was a change which *erased*
12. in *over* must have into wretchedness (gloom *above line*) *erased before* Despondence
18. the offer *for* they
19. advantageous *for* favourable

6. at *added above line before* Croydon
8. It is a pity you should not go *erased after* kind to you
9. off *added above line after* worse
12. you *added above line before* think for
15. esteem *for* affection

A SUPPRESSED PASSAGE

The following passage was cancelled. For the passage which replaced it, see the notes on pages 79–80.

As every word is erased, the distinction between the first draft and alterations is in some degree a matter of conjecture.

You mean (I am to suppose *above line*) a compliment of course my Lord, said Emma bowing, tho' I do (can *above line*) not exactly understand (define *above line*) it." Lord Osborne laughed rather awkwardly—& then said " Upon my soul, I am a bad one for Compliments. Nobody can be a worse hand at it (such things *above line*) than myself." (I wish I knew more of the matter *above line*) and after some minutes silence—added, " Can (not *above line*) you give me a lesson Miss Watson on the art of paying Comp^{ts}—I should be very glad to learn." I want very much to know how to please the Ladies—one Lady at least (A cold monosyllable & grave look from Emma repressed the growing *above line*) freedom of his manner He had too much sence, not to take the hint—& when he spoke again, it was with a degree of courteous propriety which he had never used before. (was not often at *above line*) the trouble of using (employing. *above line*) He was rewarded

VARIATIONS IN THE EDITION OF 1871

The 1871 text of *The Watsons*—unlike that of *Lady Susan*—is almost free from injudicious modernization. It contains, however, a number of errors, of which some are serious. The worst of these is at p. 7 (of this edition), where the sentiment ' I could do very well single for my own part ' is attributed to Emma Watson instead of to her sister. The following may also be noted :

Page 1 l. 5. county *for* Country
Page 12 l. 13. somebody *for* something
Page 19 l. 22. four *for* two
Page 21 l. 16. her mother, who had brought her up *for* the Mother who had brought her up
Page 23 l. 2. many other little articles *for* every other little article
Page 24 l. 15. was *for* were
Page 28 l. 12. anxiety *for* curiosity
Page 29 l. 18. them, it did not suit *omitted*
Page 36 l. 6. the young *for* the young Men
Page 39 l. 15. considering *for* wondering
Page 45 l. 7. exclaim delightedly *for* delightedly whisper
Page 46 l. 8. tea *for* ten
Page 47 l. 15. Mʳ H. *omitted*
Page 48 l. 13. determined *for* determining
Page 50 l. 22. more *omitted*
Page 54 l. 2. me *for* us
Page 65 l. 20. He *for* That he
Page 70 l. 18. being *for* becoming
Page 71 l. 17. spread them *for* spread
Page 78 l. 1. companion *for* neighbour
Page 81 l. 7. tell Betty to *omitted*
Page 85 l. 7. their security *for* this serenity
Page 93 l. 15. a stranger *for* the Stranger
Page 95 l. 16. to her the power *for* to herself the power & the pleasure

NOTES

Page 99 l. 20. he *for* we
Page 103 l. 6. seated *for* sitting
Page 104 l. 19. rational *for* national
Page 105 l. 16. sharply *for* smartly
Page 107 l. 6 and 108 l. 2. was *for* were
Page 109 l. 2. could *for* would
Page 112 l. 22. stile of *omitted*
Page 113 l. 12. would have to *for* must
Page 114 l. 2. happy ? *for* happy. (construction misunderstood ?)
Page 115 l. 4. her *for* her feelings
Page 116 l. 13. beyond calculation *for* beyond her calculation
Page 118 l. 9. mind and dissipation *for* mind, the dissipation
Page 119 l. 4. affections *for* affection

At page 60 l. 22 the 1871 edition reads ' as his road lay quite wide from D.' This was a legitimate editorial change ; but it obscured the interesting fact that in this place Miss Austen wrote not D. but R., and did not alter it. As the only town in Surrey of which the full name is given is Guildford, it is natural to think of D as Dorking and of R as Reigate.